Donna

Quixote

GLENYS YAFFE

Cover Design by BookPOD
Printed and bound in Australia by BookPOD

A Cataloguing-in-Publication entry is available from the National Library of Australia

ISBN: 978-1-925457-00-1 (pbk.)
eISBN: 978-1-925457-01-8

Acknowledgements

Thank you to my family and friends, who have been a source of support and patience during the time I've engaged in my writing adventure, whether by reading and providing feedback along the way, or by just being there whilst I've de-briefed and unloaded my frustrations, writer's blocks and excitement; you have been invaluable in this wonderful process.

Thank you to my Writers' Group at Phoenix Park, for being my valued critics and fellow travellers. And especially to Nicole Hayes, our leader, teacher and inspiration. Your comments and guidance have provided a very special foundation of encouragement and learning.

Thank you to Lee Kofman, who provided me with such helpful mentoring advice in the early stages of writing this book.

Thank you also to Ray Mooney, who was my original teacher, and gave me the confidence to engage in what has become my source of nourishment and delight.

And thank you to Sylvie & Michael Blair from BookPOD, for helping me finally bring this labour of love to fruition.

Chapter 1

Donna stared into the mirror. She didn't look too bad. Maybe it was just that she was in a good light. You couldn't see the wrinkles. Pity she couldn't take this light with her wherever she went!

Her eyes were her best feature, big and brown. She made the most of them, carefully applying eyeliner to accentuate their almond shape. She thought about what she should wear. That plum dress was always a winner; it hid lots of body flaws. The old body wasn't what it used to be. No more tiny eighteen inch waist (what was that in centremetres again?) accentuating her full breasts. She looked at her breasts now; they'd sagged since those days. But then, a good bra worked wonders. She stood side on to the mirror. Her butt was still okay. She sucked her tummy in. She probably should get back to the gym. Still, not too bad for a sixty-year-old.

Another birthday. Truth was, she'd been feeling pretty cheerless about turning sixty. Where the hell had the years gone? She sighed, putting the finishing touches to her makeup. Trudy and Alan, her closest friends, would be here to pick her up soon to take her out to dinner, together with her daughter Becky and her husband, James. Pity Luke couldn't be here. But that's what happens when your son decides to live across the other side of the world. She'd hoped he'd have called her for her birthday. Come to think of it, it had been a while since she'd heard from him. Donna sighed. It hurt a bit. But then, she knew his life was busy.

She was looking forward to a good night. It was just the acknowledgement that she'd hit the big six-oh that was difficult to accept. Despite her qualms about celebrating this milestone, though, she'd been pleased when Trudy had called a few weeks ago, asking what she wanted to do.

For a moment her mind had drifted back to her fiftieth. How different things were then. Martin had made her a surprise party. Fifty people were waiting in her favourite restaurant. He'd booked the place out, invited everyone and arranged the whole thing, somehow managing to keep it all a secret. She'd expected a dinner for two and was blown away to see how he'd managed the whole thing. She'd always been their social manager, so she was thrilled he'd managed to do all that for her.

But things had changed. Within two years her marriage had ended. No point in going back there, though.

She'd thought about Trudy and Alan's offer to organise something for her, and what she'd like this time. She decided she'd prefer a small gathering, with the people she felt closest to and who had been there for her through the rough times. Besides, it would be just after New Year's Eve, and one big party was enough.

Her friendship with Trudy and Alan went back nearly forty-five years, she realised with a shock. Forty-five years! They'd hung out in the same crowd as teenagers. Well, what do they say? People come into our lives for a reason, a season or a lifetime. She was definitely hanging onto these two for the lifetime.

Alan was now also her boss; she worked in his medical practice. It had been a lifesaver when he'd offered her the job nine months ago. She needed to get back into the workforce to retain her sanity, and didn't feel like going back into HR. She'd been away from it for too long. Besides, she wanted a change of scenery, something completely disconnected from her past. And Alan had come to the rescue, yet again.

Good old Alan. She knew he could have found someone who had experience in a medical practice, but he was looking after her, as always. He and Trudy had been a great source of support throughout these difficult years. She was pleased to be celebrating with them tonight.

She glanced at the clock. Seven twenty-five. They'd be here any moment. She turned out the light in her bedroom and made her way downstairs.

She didn't know what she would have done without their friendship. It had been Trudy who had found her a few years back, slumped across her bed, empty pill bottle not far away. Now she was relieved that her friend had had a key to her house. She hadn't thought that at the time, of course; in fact she'd felt angry that she hadn't just been left to die. Twenty-eight years of marriage. Finished. Just like that. She'd always seen herself as a strong woman, but she'd sunk into a deep depression.

It took Donna a long time to get over the sense of betrayal. She'd thought she and Martin had a good marriage. Had she missed out on something? She'd always assumed they were solid as a rock. Not quite joined at the hip, but they did most things together. Donna thought Martin had liked that. He never hinted that he wasn't happy.

So it came as a complete shock that night he'd come home, sat her down and poured a stiff whisky for them both. His face looked tired and drawn. Must have been a particularly hard day at work today, she'd thought, waiting for him to unburden, as he had always done during their years together.

Martin sat for a long time before talking. He took a deep breath. 'Donna, there's something I have to tell you.'

She noticed he looked pale, and he said nothing for a couple more minutes.

'What's happened?'

'Donna...' He hesitated. 'This is so hard. I don't know how to say this but...look, you know what, there's no easy way to tell you.' He paused. 'I'm... leaving you.'

No, she hadn't heard right. 'What are you talking about? I...we're good...we've...always been good.'

The room started spinning, and everything felt surreal. Martin was silent. She looked across at him, panic setting in.

7

Finally he spoke. 'We've had great years together. You've been a good wife and a good mother. I'm so sorry. I hate hurting you. It's...I've met someone else.'

Donna couldn't talk. Her words seemed to stick in her throat; it was like those nightmares where you try to scream and nothing comes out. Surely if she waited a moment the nightmare would end. Everything would go back to normal. Then she heard her own racking sobs filling the room, and her desperate words. 'Who is she? Why? I don't understand. If...if you think I've been a good wife...we've been good together...why?'

'Donna, I never intended this. Sometimes these things just happen.'

"Sometimes these things just happen". She replayed his words now in her mind. No, they didn't just happen, arsehole. You let them happen. You never did take responsibility for that. She breathed deeply. She'd thought she was over it all. Over him leaving her for someone gorgeous and fifteen years younger than her. After all, it had been eight years ago. But sometimes the feelings just came flooding back. Like a tidal wave. Still, she was stronger now, and the impact of the tidal wave didn't last so long.

Sometimes she even found herself thinking now *she*, Trisha the bitch, was welcome to him. When she'd seen him last he'd grown quite podgy, and his black hair had become grey and sparse. If she was honest, she'd never found him all that attractive physically. But he had a good mind, and she'd always found him fascinating to talk to. She wondered if Trisha could talk to him like that too. Probably didn't matter as long as she kept him happy in bed.

The doorbell cut across her thoughts.

'Happy birthday, darling.' Alan and Trudy burst into a chorus of "Happy Birthday to you" as she opened the door.

'So, old girl, how does it feel to be...?' Alan laughed as he substituted mumbles for "sixty".

'Enough of that "old girl" stuff,' she responded.

They hugged, and made their way to the car.

~~

Becky and James were already sitting at the table as they entered the restaurant. Donna felt a warm glow. She was pleased she'd opted for this. She didn't feel so comfortable in large crowds any more. Her confidence had been shattered. She didn't like it, but knew that was the collateral damage. She sometimes wondered if she'd ever completely return to the Donna of old. What had happened to that vivacious, carefree woman, the witty hostess who loved to be surrounded by people? Sometimes now she felt the vitality had all been drained out of her and she'd been left with an empty shell. Still, she knew the embers of her old self were there somewhere; she just needed to find a way to restore that *joie de vivre*.

Now she revelled in the hugs and good wishes, then, on everyone's insistence, started unwrapping her presents. She'd thought it would be better to wait till she got home rather than litter the restaurant with gift-wrap, but they wouldn't hear of it.

She started unwrapping a green rectangular gift first. When she undid that she uncovered a red layer. She smiled at Becky. They did this sometimes, a playful activity reminiscent of the parcel game they'd played at their birthday parties as children. When she got to the last layer, she found an envelope with a beautiful card made by her grandchildren, together with a gift voucher. Becky and James, together with Luke and his partner Jacquie, had arranged a two-day stay for her at a B&B overlooking the water in Lorne. Lorne had been a favourite family holiday spot for years. This treat was an indulgence she wouldn't have given herself, and they knew it.

She must email Luke to thank him. She was glad he hadn't forgotten, even if he hadn't called. She felt tears come to her eyes for a moment, but quickly pushed them away. She never used to get weepy like this. Trudy gently touched her arm. She didn't miss much.

She blew them kisses across the table, then turned her attention to the second gift, unwrapping it.

'Trudy, you shouldn't have!' she cried out with delight.

Trudy had been with her when she'd admired a delicate rose quartz necklace a couple of weeks ago; at the time she'd been tempted to buy it. In the end she knew that it was an extravagant spend, and decided to be more sensible. She put it on now, her cheeks flushed from the excitement of her gifts and her pleasure at being here with her loved ones.

'Okay, what are we going to eat?' Alan asked. 'I'm starving. I didn't have lunch today because I wanted to save it all for tonight. I hear the calamari's good.'

They perused the menu, and made their choices. Donna decided, 'I'm going to be daring and go for oysters naturale. God, I never thought I'd ever be able to try oysters that weren't disguised with cheese or some sort of sauce. Gotta make some changes and put some spark into my life. Live dangerously while I can. And then I'll have the duck a l'orange. Yum, my mouth is watering. I'm hungry, too.'

Throughout dinner Donna felt grateful: wine, good food and people who love you. What more could anyone want? *Relish the moment.* That's what Norm, her therapist, kept reminding her.

~~

They'd finished their main course. James was looking at his watch. 'I'm getting fidgety. I won't wait for desserts. I hate to break up the party, but I've got a phone call coming through from New York. How about I get a cab home, and you can stay, Beck, and give your Mum a lift home.'

'Okay,' Becky replied. 'It'll give me a chance to talk to her about something.'

Donna glanced at her daughter, wondering what the "something" was she wanted to talk about. But she could tell Becky was not going to be drawn out about it now.

~~

They were half way home when Becky said, 'Mum, I've been thinking…'

Donna looked suspiciously at her daughter. There was something in her tone that she wasn't sure about. A tentative, unusual wavering of her voice.

'Yes?' An equally tentative response.

'James and I were talking the other night. Do you think about whether maybe…maybe you'd like to meet someone else now?'

Donna felt herself flush. She hadn't expected they'd consider that. They had busy lives, and she wouldn't have imagined it would ever occur to them she might like a new partner. She thought they just saw her as an aging grandma. But it had actually been on her mind lately, too. She sometimes felt lonely, and was starting to consider how nice it would be to have someone in her life again.

'Where am I'm going to meet anyone else? You can't hang out at bars at my stage of life. And no gorgeous guys seem to cross my path these days.'

'Ever thought about going on One Plus One?' Becky asked.

Donna stared at her daughter. 'Me? On one of those internet sites? I'm too old to be doing that sort of thing.'

Becky ignored the age issue, but responded with, 'I'll help you to put together a profile.'

'I don't know if I could do it. I wouldn't know where to start.'

'I'll come over next weekend. I'm busy this week, but how about next Sunday?'

God, she's persistent, thought Donna. 'We'll talk about it,' she responded after a moment.

Could she actually consider relating to a man again? Hell, Martin was the only man she'd ever been with. Would she be able to get used to being with someone new? What would it be like to let another man see her sixty-year-old body? It felt scary. She felt a nervous knot in her stomach. But there was something exciting about the idea, too.

They'd arrived home. She opened the car door.

Becky waved. 'See you next Sunday.' It seemed she was determined not to be put off.

Donna went inside. It was quiet. Too quiet. This is when it seemed to hit her most. After being out somewhere, and coming back to the stillness. Donna went to put some music on. She felt in a Rod Stewart sort of mood. She selected one of his Great American Songbook albums, a favourite CD, and poured herself a Bailey's over ice. Maybe One Plus One wasn't such a crazy idea. But...

She settled back into the couch, and sipped her drink. She'd talk to the girls about it over lunch tomorrow. She hoped they'd all be there. What was it now? Fifteen years since it all began. First Saturday of the month.

Chapter 2

Donna liked Rick's Cafe. It had a buzzy ambience that nourished her vicariously; she was an incurable people-watcher. Its slightly quirky, put-together décor with table cloths that didn't always match, and its enticing menu drew a pot-pourri of people of varying ages ranging from arty through to corporate types. But despite the busyness of the café it wasn't one of those noisy places that drowned out conversation. She loved her monthly D&M's with her friends, and they'd all been through so much together over the years.

Thank goodness she'd gone to that school reunion. If not, the "first Saturday" group would never have happened. She'd been delighted to see Paula there again. They'd been best friends during those years at school. Paula had been the fairly quiet, studious one in those days, while Donna tended to be more outgoing. Still, they hit it off from the start, and the friendship blossomed right through their high school years. But after they finished her friend had gone on to study architecture at Melbourne, while Donna had gone to Monash to do an arts degree. That was probably part of why they'd drifted apart. And Paula was engrossed in her relationship with Mike then; so their lives had taken off in different directions.

For a few years they met sporadically, then their meetings dropped right off. When they saw each other again all those years later, though, the in-between time seemed to dissolve.

The reunion had been held in a hall of the old school. Paula had spotted her as soon as she entered the room. 'Donna!' she called, obviously pleased to see her. She almost ran across the room and gave her old school friend a hug. 'How many years has it been? You still look just like I remember you.'

'Just a few more curves and wrinkles,' Donna chuckled.

'It can't be more than twenty five years since we did Year 12 here,' said Paula. 'And probably ten years since we saw each other.'

'Yes, it must be. And how is Mike?'

'I don't know. We're divorced.' Her face dropped. "I found out he'd been having affairs for years and in the end I couldn't bear it any more.'

'Ouch. That must have hurt like hell. How long have you been divorced?'

'It's five years now.'

'Anyone else in your life?'

'No. I don't think I could do it again. Can't imagine anyone wanting me, to be honest, and it feels too scary to put myself out there. If my own husband didn't find me attractive…'

'Oh Paula, don't do that to yourself. You've got so much to offer the right man.' She knew, even as she said it, that Paula wouldn't believe her. She'd always had difficulty recognising her qualities. 'You always did lack confidence.'

'Yeah, I know.' Paula shrugged. 'Anyway, I've got my work, and life's pretty good all round.'

'And Fran? How's she?'

'She's great. She's just started studying Vet Science, and she's loving it.'

'No way. Fran at Uni? Boy, nothing like our kids to remind us the years are passing. Of course you started earlier than me. You were a child bride,' Donna laughed.

The next couple of hours passed quickly, as they filled each other in on the missing years. When it was time to leave they agreed to catch up for lunch soon. After that they made a regular habit of setting aside the first Saturday of each month to meet.

'I'm not going to let you drift out of my life again,' Paula had told her.

One by one others had been invited to join their lunch group, as women they thought might enjoy and add to their lunches were

14

included; over the following few years their group of two became six. And they'd barely missed their monthly lunch in all those years.

Now there were five left. They'd all been pretty cut up when Gina died a few months ago. Fifty-five was much too young to go. The group had been through the phases of hope and despair as their friend struggled through chemotherapy and radiotherapy. They'd all hoped that she'd come through it like Halle, one of the others in their group, who'd survived breast cancer a few years earlier. But in the end it wasn't to be.

It had been painful for them to see Gina's deterioration during the few short months between diagnosis and death. Especially with someone like Gina. She'd been a stunning woman. Nearly six feet tall, attractive, proud, vain, and independent. Impending death the leveller, Donna thought, sadly. They all saw how Gina had battled against her increasing dependence on others as she became more frail. Donna wished her friend could have reached more of a sense of peace and acceptance about her imminent death. But knowing Gina, that wasn't ever going to happen. In life she'd always taken control of everything. She couldn't do that with death!

Donna missed her a lot. Sometimes she still expected her to walk into the room, with one of her witty one-liners. She made her way to their usual table in the corner.

Trudy was already there. And Paula and Halle. Donna noticed presents on the table, and was embarrassed. She'd never been very good at accepting things from others. It was so much easier to give than receive. But at the same time she felt pleased they were acknowledging her birthday. She had to admit to herself she would have been disappointed if they hadn't made some fuss over her. Even if she did have her concerns about turning sixty.

'Happy Birthday,' they chorused as she sat down.

'Welcome to the world of the "wise woman",' Halle laughed. She had celebrated her sixtieth just over a year ago in grand form, on a boat, with champagne flowing and waiters offering finger food all night. But that was what they'd have expected for Halle; it was part of her lifestyle. She worked as an events manager, and was used to organising corporate functions.

Donna smiled and shrugged at her friend's comment. 'Wise woman? I don't know about that. I feel like I'm just hitting middle age, and far from wise,' she responded.

'Hi everyone.' A voice echoed across the restaurant announcing the arrival of Nina, the bohemian of the group. Her flowing bright blue top and vibrant red curls ensured she could not go unnoticed. She was the quintessential artist, eccentric, feisty, and always entertaining. Her life was a series of happenings and mishaps, and they always enjoyed hearing about them. Donna tried to remember how Nina had become one of the group. Ah yes, it had been through Gina.

'Happy Birthday, darling,' she called as she approached the table. She was the "baby" among them at forty-one.

'Well, we're a full house,' said Paula.

~~

An hour had gone by. The women were through their main course and trying to make up their minds if their figures could tolerate desserts.

'I think I could force myself to have the Chocolate Mousse,' said Nina.

'That's okay for you. Look at you, pencil slim, legs up to your neck,' said Paula. 'It's fatty-boombas like me who have to worry about it.'

Paula was always worrying about her weight.

'You do exaggerate, Paula. You might be carrying a few extra kilos, but this is more about your self-esteem than about being overweight,' argued Nina.

Paula sighed. She wasn't convinced. Donna glanced across at her friend. Of course Paula had always lacked confidence, as far back as she could remember. And she had gained some weight, which had compounded her self doubt. But that wasn't the main issue. She seemed to have aged a few years in a short time, and though they were chronologically almost identical, Paula now looked years older. She had an attractive face, but it was tinged now with sadness, with a look that suggested her spark had been extinguished. Well, an only child's death would do that, wouldn't it? Donna shuddered, not wanting to contemplate what that must be like. They'd all tried to support their friend in whatever ways they could since that terrible night when Fran had been wiped out by that alcohol-fuelled idiot who had slammed into her car.

Paula had been strong. Too strong, Donna often thought. But deep down that terrible event had eaten away at an already fragile psyche, and Paula seemed lacking any real vitality since that time.

Donna wiped away a tear. It always distressed her when she thought about what Paula had been through. She looked around at her friends, chatting and engrossed in conversation.

'Pity we can't ever find enough to talk about,' Halle laughed.

'Yeah, it's the dull lives we live,' Nina responded.

~~

There was a temporary lull in the conversation. Donna decided she'd like to raise the idea of One Plus One to see what the others thought of the idea. She was surprised how nervous she was to broach the subject. After all, they'd talked about pretty well everything on the planet over these years. She knew it was because she was feeing unsure about it herself.

'You won't believe what Becky wants me to do,' she said, blushing a little. She couldn't believe she was blushing. Or that it was such a big deal. 'She actually wants me to try internet dating. How about that?' She was aware she'd put an edge of ridicule to the idea in case they thought it foolish. She waited for someone to respond.

'Sounds like a good idea to me. How do you feel about it?' asked Halle.

'Well…I was afraid I was too old to be doing that sort of thing. You reckon it sounds okay?'

Paula laughed. 'Didn't I ever tell you how I met Ted? We met through One Plus One.'

'You're joking.' Donna stared at her friend. 'I never knew that.'

Paula had met Ted, her second husband, just over a couple of years ago. So she was also close to sixty when she'd tried the internet. Donna was silent for a moment. 'That makes me feel better. Because after I'd discounted the idea I actually found myself feeling excited at the possibility. I just didn't know if people our age did that sort of thing.'

'I didn't either,' replied Paula. 'And I would never have had the guts to do it, but my young sister Chrissie dobbed me in. She put my profile up without me knowing, and then told me. She knew I'd never have agreed to it unless it was a *fait accompli*. I was annoyed at first, but then reluctantly decided to give it a go. I would never have met Ted without her manipulation! You'd be amazed. There's lots of us. And although there are more women, there are lots of men who'd also love to meet someone.'

'Yes, but plenty who just want some casual sex, too,' said Trudy. 'We're going to have to vet them for you. No bastard's going to get his hands on our mate!'

Donna laughed. 'You make it sound like they're going to be beating down my door to meet me. You…you think there might be a chance for this old girl to meet someone?'

'Yes, there's every chance. And you're going to have some fun along the way,' Trudy said.

'It could be exciting,' said Nina. 'Maybe I'll give it a go, too. We can compare notes.'

'Yeah, well it would be good for you to find someone who's not married like Tony is, that's for sure. That's a dead end,' said Trudy.

Nina just shrugged, without responding. She'd heard it all before. God knows she already knew it.

Chapter 3

The doorbell rang. Ten thirty on the dot. Becky was always punctual. Like me, Donna thought. She couldn't bear to be late, and it seemed she'd instilled the same habits in her daughter.

'I'm quite excited, but I do feel nervous about this whole idea,' Donna said, as they settled in the study.

'I checked out a few profiles of women in your age range just to get some idea of what to include,' Becky offered, 'and I also spoke to a friend who's been on One Plus One for a while now, and she gave me a few clues. But if you don't like anything I suggest, we can change it.'

Donna watched her log onto the One Plus One site.

'First thing we need is a name,' Becky informed her.

'A name? What do you mean?'

'You need a pseudonym for your profile.'

Donna thought for a minute. 'How about *Dollybelle?*' she suggested. 'It's what Grandpa used to call me sometimes.'

'Yuk, no. Unless you want to attract the dorks or people of Grandpa's age. Hm, let's see.' She laughed. 'You could be *Prissymissy.*'

'But never *Kiss and Tell.*'

'How about *Lascivious Lady?*' Becky joked.

They both burst into laughter.

'Or *La Bella Cruella?*'

'Then you'd better get your whips and leathers out of the closet.'

'Should I be talking to my daughter like this?'

'Why not? You always have.'

They continued to play with names.

'Stop, my sides are aching from laughing so much,' said Donna after a while.

'You look like a young girl when you giggle like that. It's great to see you laughing again.'

They continued to bounce names off each other.

'Any more suggestions? I've run out of ideas,' Donna asked.

'What about something like *CheekyChic?*'

'Yes, that sounds like me.'

'Okay, *CheekyChic* it is.' Becky typed it in. 'Now have a look at this. Here are some ideas that I put together last night. How does this sound?

Are you my man? A George Clooney look-alike, with the brain of Einstein?'

'Yes, that's a neat opener.' Donna smiled.

'Then I thought you could say,

Always ready to bring me that first cup of tea in bed?

In return, I may pour your drinks and have the fire going when you come home, and we'll sit and listen to anything from Beethoven to Beatles, depending on our mood. We can enjoy cooking dinner together. Then perhaps my inner child will dance with your inner child till late, before falling into bed exhausted.'

'We could add *but not too exhausted*,' suggested Donna, chuckling.

'I like that. Then let's say,

I am an intelligent, honest, kind woman; you'll find I'm also loyal, generous and affectionate.'

'Hm. I don't feel comfortable describing myself like that. It feels a bit bold.'

Becky laughed. 'That's so like you. But we can change that. How about,

My children and friends describe me as intelligent, honest, kind...etc?'

'Okay. That sounds better.'

'Let's add,

With just a touch enough mischief to keep you on your toes.'

'Yes, okay.'

'How does this sound?' asked Becky.

If you insist we go to five star hotels and have dinner at a three hat restaurant every other week, you can persuade me. But I'll also be happy to help you pitch a tent by the side of some beautiful country spot, or by the water.'

'Yes, that's good.'

'Then maybe we should say something about how funny you can be. How about something like,

You'll love my wicked sense of humour, and I'll enjoy making you smile. And your wit will warm my heart. But we'll also be able to cry together at sad movies.'

'Mm. Yes, that sounds okay, too. Then, how about,

So if you are a sincere, gentle, intelligent and caring man who is not afraid to share his feelings, why not contact me?'

'Okay?' she asked Becky.

'Yes. And we could finish up with,

Together we could make our lives an exciting journey. I look forward to meeting you.'

Becky looked across at her mother. 'You're looking a lot more relaxed now.' Donna nodded.

'What sort of age range do you want to look for?' asked Becky.

'Hm. Maybe fifty eight to sixty five?' She laughed. 'You reckon I'll get any toy-boys answering?'

'You never know your luck.'

The two of them then went through the process of adding the additional information requested: what sorts of music, film and TV shows she liked, what physical activities and sport, etc.

'And they also ask about eye and hair colour, and body type.'

'Ugh. What do I say about my body type? Overweight with bulges in the wrong places?'

'Come on, Mum, there's nothing wrong with your body. But we could call you "voluptuous" if you like.'

Donna laughed. They'll expect they're getting some big-bosomed delight if we put that.'

'How about "curvy"?'

They continued to bounce off each other as they filled in the rest of the profile. Donna found that, to her surprise, it was already twelve thirty. 'That's taken us two hours,' she exclaimed. 'I'd better let you get home. The kids will be wondering what's happened to you.'

'It's okay. James has taken them to a movie. They'll be perfectly happy and not missing me at all.'

'Well, thanks for doing all this for me, Beck.'

'We're not finished. We need to do your photo now.'

Donna gasped. 'A photo? Do I really have to do that?'

'Yes, you do. You're much more likely to get a response with a photo. People like to have a visual picture of who they're contacting.'

'Well, there's that photo from Bonny's christening, I suppose we could use that.'

'Mum, that's five years old! You need a recent one.'

'I haven't got one. It's been ages since I had one taken.'

'Okay, I'll take one now. Go and put some makeup on.'

Donna walked quickly upstairs to her dressing room, applied her makeup, then looked at herself in the mirror. Did she look too old? She took a deep breath. Well, she decided, what you see is what you get. Okay, here goes.

She wandered back into the lounge room, where Becky was waiting. She took several snaps of her mother, and together they looked at them, selecting the one that they both liked best. A few minutes later Becky had posted it on One Plus One.

'You just have to wait for them to approve your photo now, and you'll be up and running.'

Becky spent a few more minutes going through and explaining the mechanics of the site.

'Thanks again, Beck. I'm nervous as all get-up now, seeing that all up on the computer, but I'll give it a go.'

'Good,' Becky replied, before kissing her mother's cheek and making her way to the door. 'Just wait for the "hugs" to come in now.'

Donna had already learned that "hugs" were what the initial contacts between One Plus One members were called.

'You think I'll get any responses?'

'You'll be beating them off with a stick,' laughed Becky. 'Gotta go now. Bye. Enjoy.'

Donna saw her out, then went back to the computer, reviewing what they had written. What a hoot. Well, it was done now. She'd just have to wait and see where it all took her.

Chapter 4

It had been a busy day at the clinic. Donna was looking forward to putting her feet up. She poured herself a glass of Shiraz; the bottle had been her birthday gift from Paula. She made herself comfortable, her MacBook balanced on her lap. She took a sip, then turned the laptop on with a tinge of excitement.

New mail had arrived. She had been impatient, checking her emails far more frequently than usual. A couple of days had passed since her profile had gone up. She found her heart was beating a little faster than usual. She looked through the incoming mail.

Three messages from One Plus One. Though her hands were shaking a little with nervousness, she found herself smiling. She was having fun, and was glad Becky had given her a nudge to do this.

The first message was a "hug" from someone who called himself *Lonely and Looking*. She went to his profile. Hm. She thought his email screamed of neediness. She didn't fancy that. And he was seventy-five. Too old. She was surprised people in their seventies were doing this sort of thing. And she'd thought she was already past it!

Donna minimised the first, and went to her second response.

This one came from *Randy Randy*. A thirty-five year old. Was he for real? She promptly deleted it.

She opened the third. It was an email from someone called *Pathway*. A couple of years younger than her. This one felt more like it. Almost too good to be true, she thought, reading what he'd written about himself. Sensitive, romantic, open, generous and looking for his soul-mate. Not bad looking, either.

She read his email.

Hi CheekyChic,
I've just read your profile, and think we have quite a lot in common, and are both looking for similar things. And I like the sound of your wicked sense of humour. People tell me that I have one, too. We could keep each other laughing a lot.
And yes, I do cry in sad movies!
I work in I.T. Although I live in Sydney for part of the time, I usually spend Monday to Friday in Melbourne, where my company has their head office. Things are frenetic at the moment, but I'd love us to meet when I am here next week. Any night other than Wednesday would work for me. Or if you'd rather just exchange emails for a while until I pass the test, that's okay too.
Maybe we could talk on the phone and see how we feel about that? I look forward to hearing more from you,
Warmly,
Harvey

He'd added his phone number underneath. Donna felt a warm tingle through her body. This was exciting! She hadn't known whether she'd hear from anyone she'd want to meet. It probably wasn't ideal that he was based in Sydney, but five days a week in Melbourne seemed okay. And she liked the sound of him.

Initially she thought she'd prefer to keep emailing for a while before meeting. But then she decided to dive in. If she was going to do this thing she might as well do it properly. Besides, you couldn't tell much from emails. Much better to meet face to face.

She wrote back to Harvey, saying they could meet the following Thursday night, and suggested they talk on the phone in the next couple of days to arrange where and when; then she added her own mobile number.

She looked at the clock. Her stomach was telling her it was time to eat. Something quick, she decided. She went to her fridge to check what she had there. Some broccolini, mushrooms, asparagus and prosciutto. And some lamb fillets. That should satisfy her hunger pangs. She busied herself with preparing a stir-fry, and found that she was singing as she cooked. She smiled to herself, realising it had been a while since she'd found herself singing. Nothing like the prospect of romance to cheer a woman up.

She walked to the couch, placing her dinner on the coffee table in front of her, but then decided some music and some more wine wouldn't go amiss. She felt in a mellow mood. Something classical and melodious. She found one of her Mendelsohn favourites and put that on, then settled into her meal, finishing it quickly. She felt much better now that the hunger pangs were gone.

The wine was good. She sipped slowly, closing her eyes for a few minutes.

The sound of the phone sliced through the peace of the moment. For a couple of seconds she felt disappointed to have her reverie disturbed. She picked up the phone, hoping it wasn't another one of those market research or sales calls.

She heard a man's voice, deep and sexy.

'Hello, is that Donna?'

'Yes. Who's this?'

'It's Harvey. From One Plus One.'

Donna gulped. She hadn't expected to hear from him so quickly. 'Hi.'

'I hope I haven't interrupted anything. I know you said we'd talk over the next couple of days, but I couldn't resist phoning you as soon as I got your email. I was supposed to be out tonight, but as fate would have it that was cancelled. So here I am.'

Donna could feel her heart racing. 'It's good to hear from you. And no, you didn't interrupt me. I've just finished dinner, and was relaxing and listening to some music.'

'Yes, I can hear it. Sounds like Mendelsohn's violin concerto. It happens to be one of my favourites.' He paused. 'Good start, hey? We both like the same music.'

Donna laughed. 'Yes, perhaps it's a sign.'

They talked for another half an hour. Donna was pleasantly surprised at how the conversation flowed; he was so easy to speak to.

Then Harvey said, 'So, next Thursday we have a date? I'd love to take you to dinner. Where would you like to go?'

'Well, probably depends where you're coming from. Where are you staying? I live in Elwood, so maybe we can meet half way?'

'I've got an apartment in Fitzroy. Since I'm down here so much it seemed to make sense to get myself a place here rather than going to hotels or serviced apartments. But I don't mind where we meet. Do you have a favourite place? What sort of food do you like?'

'I love Italian or French. Or Japanese. But I eat most food.'

'Want me to pick a place?'

'Yes, that would be great.'

Donna wasn't used to choosing restaurants, or going out on dates, so she liked that he'd suggested this.

'Okay. What about somewhere by the water? That's always lovely at this time of the year.'

'Sounds perfect.'

Harvey suggested a few places, and finally they settled on Franco's Bistro, which was a place Donna had eaten at several times, and had especially enjoyed.

'Do you want me to pick you up?'

Donna had already been told quite emphatically by Trudy that she must arrange to meet men somewhere, rather than reveal her address, at least until she got to know them. Harvey sounded okay, but she heeded her friend's advice, and replied, 'Thanks, but no, this first time I'd prefer to meet you there.'

'Okay, I understand. See you at Franco's at say 7.30? Does that suit you?'

'Yes, sounds good.'

'I look forward to it. Good night, and sleep well.'

Donna hung up. She felt too excited to settle yet, and picked up the phone again, calling Trudy.

'I've just arranged to go on a date.'

'Already? That's great. But you'd better tell me all about him. We're not going to let you go out with any creeps, remember. Will he pass the Trudy and Alan test?'

Donna laughed. 'He sounds nice. I think he'll pass.'

She relayed the main threads of their conversation to her friend before saying goodnight. She put another CD on, and sat back, listening and contemplating the evening.

Chapter 5

'This month seems to have flown,' said Nina.

They had managed to get their favourite table again. Trudy and Donna had also arrived at Rick's. No doubt the others would be there soon.

'I'm hanging out for a drink,' Nina said. It's been a hell of a week. What'll it be, one red and one white?'

'Sounds about right,' Trudy replied. 'Do you want to choose? You always do a good job of that.'

'Probably because I'm the pisspot of the group,' laughed Nina. 'Okay, what do you think, a Sauvignon Blanc and a Shiraz?'

'Yeah, that'll be good,' Trudy replied.

Nina busied herself with the drinks menu, while the others chatted. Halle and Paula arrived soon after, and the table was soon abuzz with conversation and their usual intermittent laughter.

'So why's it been a hell of a week?' Trudy asked Nina during one of the rare quieter moments.

'That guy I told you about that I met at that art exhibition. Don. He's been hanging around. I feel bad, because he's a decent guy, but I told him this week I couldn't see us having a future together. He's just been a mess. He thought we were so close, and I suppose we were for a while. I feel bad about it, but… He was on the phone last night for over an hour, and he was crying. He says he's in love with me.'

'Nina, why do I feel like I've heard this before?' said Halle.

'Yeah, I know.'

'Seems like you always back away from the ones who are available.'

Nina hesitated. 'Yes, you're probably right. Same old same old. I start to get that trapped feeling again. I know it's a pattern. I like my independence too much. I'm probably not cut out for a full-on relationship. But what am I supposed to do? I'm not cut out for a celibate life, either.' She laughed, then added, 'I've financed every course on the planet for commitment-phobes. I don't know, I probably need to see a therapist.'

'You're not available anyway while you're still hooked up with Tony,' said Halle. 'You need to give him the flick.'

Nina didn't answer. She looked pensive, then after a moment shrugged and said, 'Anyway…enough about me. What's been happening with the rest of you this month?'

'Well,' said Donna. 'I've been out on a few dates with a guy.'

'Tell us more! From One Plus One?'

'Yes. Who'd have thought?'

'What's his name? I want to hear all the gory details. No leaving any bits out, either,' laughed Nina.

'His name's Harvey. He's lovely. We've been out a few times.'

'Promising?'

'Maybe. He's good fun. We laugh a lot. He can be very funny. And…'

'Yes? What's the "and"?' asked Nina.

'Well…he's kind of attractive.'

'So have you done the bed thing?' asked Nina.

Donna laughed. Trust Nina to ask direct questions like that. 'Yes, we've done the bed thing! Gotta say I thought I'd seen the last of that. I feel like a teenager again.'

'So was it good?'

'Nina, you needn't hold back. Why don't you just ask me directly instead of beating around the bush?' Donna joked. 'Yes, it was good. Perhaps there's life in the old girl yet.'

'What's he do? Where does he live? Has he been married? Got kids? Tell us everything. You know we need all the facts. He's still got to get past us. We've got your back, you know,' Trudy added.

Donna smiled at her friends. She knew how much they cared, and how protective they'd been of her through the hard times. 'Still got some gaps in the picture. Haven't joined all the dots yet. He's in IT. Was married, but he's separated. Three children. One grandchild. He's a couple of years younger than me.'

'So far so good,' said Halle.

'Still early days,' said Donna. 'We're seeing each other again on Tuesday night. We've been going out about two or three times a week. We do have fun. He's been taking me to dinner, and a couple of times we went to a movie. I've yet to see him cry in a movie, but he assures me he does.' She smiled. 'And he got tickets for us to see an MTC play next week. Don't remember what we're gong to see, but I'm looking forward to it.'

'Do you know what night you're going?' asked Nina. 'Tony has tickets for us on Friday night. It would be a hoot if we were there the same night. I'd be able to meet your new beau.'

'Well, I don't know that I can call him my beau yet. He has potential, but the jury's still out. You won't get to meet him this week, though. We're going on Thursday night.'

'I still don't understand how Tony gets a leave pass as often as he does. Where does his wife think he is when he's out with you?' asked Halle.

Nina shrugged. 'I don't know. He's the one who is leading the double life. He probably says he's got business meetings. It's his problem to figure out the logistics.' Her face looked dark as she responded to the question.

'I'll never understand how you've stood it for so long. What is it now, six years?' said Halle. 'You know you're settling for far too little. I couldn't do it. I'd get angry if someone was having the best of both worlds like Tony is.'

'I am angry. Everything's always on his bloody terms. I can see him when it suits him, but what I want comes a poor second. I turn myself into a pretzel for him. He calls and I come running. Christ, I've never done that for anyone before. It's insane, but I don't seem to be able to walk away.' She paused.

'You're worth more than that,' said Trudy.

32

'Does he ever talk about leaving her?' Halle asked.

'Not any more. The first couple of years he did. And by the time he stopped saying it I was already hooked.'

'But you're letting the years slip away,' said Trudy.

Donna glanced at her friend. She knew what Trudy was alluding to. Trudy had had so much difficulty coming to terms with being childless. She hadn't been able to have a baby all those years ago, and she'd been through a lot of pain accepting that.

'I know that,' Nina snapped. Then she immediately softened. She knew her friends had her best interests at heart. 'I know what you're saying. I'm going to run out of time to have a family. I'm desperate to have a child, and the biological clock isn't standing still. It's almost too late now. Don't think for a moment I'm not aware of it. It's on my mind a lot, actually keeping me awake at night, and lately I've been getting so resentful. But I can't walk away. I'm just not strong enough. Not yet, anyway.'

Trudy nodded. 'It's always going to be hard to find that strength. But we don't want you to look back and say you should have left…and didn't.'

At that moment their lunches started to arrive, and there was a temporary lull in the conversation. The food was reliably good at Rick's. It was one of the reasons they kept returning to the same spot. Occasionally one of them had suggested a new venue, and they'd tried it, but always returned to their regular lunch spot. In the end they just accepted this as their regular haunt.

When they'd finished eating and resumed a more hearty conversation Nina, who had looked quite forlorn earlier, suddenly said, 'Maybe I do need to start getting out and dating more. I know I've been out with a lot of guys, but I'm too focussed on Tony. And that's a dead end. Unless I push his wife under a bus.' She grimaced, then smiled and looked at Donna. 'Maybe I'll do what you've done. But I'll just watch from the sidelines for a little while first.' She smiled wryly. 'I'm just a crazy mixed up kid. I want a relationship but I don't. Maybe that's why it's suited me in a way to be with Tony. You know, just having the part-time thing. But meanwhile the clock just keeps ticking. I've got it shoved into the "too hard" basket.' She looked at her watch. 'I'm going to have to get going soon. My mother's coming over.

'Okay. See you on the first Saturday in March, if not before,' said Donna.

The others chorused their goodbyes.

~~

Donna got into her car, a safe, conventional Volvo, a relic from her married days. Martin had thought it was a good family car for them to have, even though by then they were no longer a nuclear family of four. The kids were grown up. But Donna hadn't questioned him.

He didn't drive a station wagon of course. The sporty Lexus was more appropriate for a man that needed to be seen as successful. But hers didn't need to be flash. Conservative silver grey.

Maybe it was a good time to consider a new car. Perhaps it could stand as a symbol for a new life. She breathed a sigh of pleasure, enjoying her fantasy of something flash. A Maserati. Well, if she could let herself play with fantasies, why not? Or a Porsche?

She emitted a sardonic laugh that reduced her fantasy to something more attainable. Perhaps a Toyota or a Honda. She flicked through various possibilities in her mind. It would need to be colourful. Maybe red? No, seemed too much like a mid-life crisis choice. Perhaps a bright yellow similar to Becky's. No, that wasn't on. She couldn't mimic a desired youthfulness. In the end she imagined a blue Mini Cooper like one she'd seen that day.

She turned left and drove into her driveway.

Chapter 6

It was Tuesday night and Donna was getting ready for Harvey to arrive. She enjoyed the slight feeling of butterflies that occurred each time they were to meet.

She reflected back on her conversation with Trudy earlier that day.

'How long has he been separated?' her friend had asked.

'I'm not sure. I didn't ask him. Why, do you think it's important?'

'Yes, I do. If he's just barely out of his marriage it could be a problem. I'm not saying it is, but I'd feel better if you asked. I don't want you getting too involved if he's still got stuff going on about his wife. And do you know why it ended?'

'No, I don't. I hadn't thought to check these things out. I need to ask more questions.' She laughed. 'I'm not used to this singles scene.'

Now she brought her attention back to getting ready. Taking great care, she went through the clothes in her cupboard, trying to decide which dress she'd wear tonight. Probably the good old faithful plum one. As she flicked through her clothing, she thought it wouldn't be a bad idea to buy herself a few new outfits. After all, she was earning money now that she was working again, and it was a long time since she'd refreshed her wardrobe. But then she had splurged yesterday. She smiled, as she took the new set of lingerie out of her drawer. It had been so long since she'd given a damn what she was wearing under her clothes, she thought, smiling to herself and enjoying the thrill of putting on the sexy outfit she'd bought: first the panties and then the bra.

Donna examined herself in the mirror. She could see curves where there weren't supposed to be curves; but Harvey seemed to like the way she looked. She'd never imagined she could get such a thrill from selecting and wearing seductive black lingerie.

She wondered if that was where she went wrong with Martin. Maybe she stopped trying to look sexy for him. But then she decided that was the last thing she wanted to have on her mind half an hour before Harvey was due to arrive for dinner.

She looked at herself again in the mirror. She could have sworn the face looking back at her seemed younger than she was used to seeing. She smiled again. Marvellous what a charming, red hot lover can do. Sighing contentedly, she slipped into her dress, and went downstairs to pour a drink for herself.

She turned the light dimmer down to a romantic low, then went to the kitchen to check the lamb shanks in the oven. They looked good, and the aroma was great. Entrée was all ready in the fridge: she'd bought some oysters, cooked prawn tails, smoked salmon, artichokes, sun dried tomatoes, and just a few Kalamata olives to scatter on the platter. Just the lemon wedges to add to the entrée, and she was all set to go. She felt a satisfied relief as she checked everything out.

This was the first time Harvey would be coming to dinner at her house. In fact it was the first time for years anyone other than her family or Trudy and Alan had been to dinner. It had made Donna realise how out of the habit of entertaining she'd become. She and Martin used to have a lot of dinner parties, and she'd taken them in her stride. But after he left the last thing she wanted to do was to worry about cooking for anyone. And she rarely felt inspired to cook anything exotic for herself. She felt out of practice. So she'd been a little nervous, but invited him anyway.

One last look at the dining room table, and she was satisfied everything was under control. She put an Il Divo disc on, and settled herself on the couch with her wine.

When she finished her glass, she glanced at her watch. Seven forty. Harvey was ten minutes late. She'd found this was a habit she was having to get used to. He was always running late. She tried to shrug this off, reprimanding herself for her rigid attention to punctuality. She told herself that given that everything else was going so smoothly this was a small price to pay.

Nevertheless, when another ten minutes had passed without any sign of him, she started to get edgy. The phone rang at eight o'clock. It was Harvey, apologising for being late.

'I've been delayed. Sorry,' he told her, 'but I couldn't get away. I should be there in ten.'

Donna was grateful that it didn't much matter with the lamb shanks, they'd just be more likely to be deliciously falling off the bone. She shrugged; she didn't want a small matter like this to take away from the pleasure of being with him.

~~

The doorbell rang. Harvey was dressed in grey, a casual sports jacket, and a very pale grey shirt. His clothes accentuated the blueness of his eyes. He looked great. Donna felt slightly breathless as he smiled at her, and drew her towards him.

'Hi, beautiful. I'm so sorry I'm late. I had an overseas call and just couldn't get away. Hope these make up for it,' he added, giving her a beautiful bunch of lilies. 'And here's some bubbly I thought you might enjoy. It's one of my favourites from the Yarra Valley.' He smiled. 'Hope dinner isn't burned.'

Donna smiled, taking the flowers and arranging them in a vase. 'Do you want to open the bubbly while I do this. And no, fortunately it's a dinner that just gets better with time.'

'Like you do.'

Donna felt a warm wave through her body. 'Just imagine how well-cooked I'll be in another few months,' she laughed. Interesting, she thought, that she obviously expected he'd still be around in a few months.

Harvey opened the bubbly, and they settled into the cosiness of the evening. One drink later, she asked, 'Ready to eat?'

'Not quite.' He leaned over to her and kissed her. Slow, and sensual.

'Mm. That feels good,' she told him.

'Plenty more to come,' he promised her. 'But first, food for sustenance. I'm *really* hungry. I didn't get time for lunch today. Better watch out, I'll eat anything…including you.' He smiled at her, then drew her close to him again. She could feel his body becoming aroused as he held her and kissed her.

'Decision time. Dinner? Or the "bed thing"?' he asked. They both laughed. Harvey had been amused when she'd told him about Nina's forthright questions.

'Depends what you're hungriest for,' she replied, running her fingers down his back. 'But you'd better put into the equation whether dinner will in fact start to get overcooked.'

'Okay.' Harvey had a look on his face of mock disappointment. 'I'll have to wait and have my dessert later. My mum always told me I had to eat all my dinner before I could have the sweet stuff. But I'm a patient man.'

'You don't feel that patient,' she teased him.

He laughed, picked her up, and carried her to the kitchen. 'Get my dinner, woman, before I ravish you on the kitchen table.'

Donna got the entrée platter out of the fridge, and they settled at the table enjoying the flavours. She got pleasure out of watching Harvey relishing the food.

'Okay, ready for the main course?' she asked when they'd finished the entrée and had a little while to digest what they'd eaten.

'Yes. Smells great. What are we having?'

'Lamb shanks with mashed potato and asparagus,' she informed him.

'My God, woman, you give me my favourite music, and now my favourite food. I *love* lamb shanks.'

'Good. Would you like one or two?'

38

'Two please. They smell delicious.'

Donna served up their dinner, and came back to the table. The meal was intermittently dotted with bits of silence while they devoured their food, with animated conversation between mouthfuls.

When they were halfway through mains, Donna asked him, 'How long have you been separated?'

She thought she saw an uncomfortable look momentarily dart across his face, but then thought maybe she was imagining it, or just looking for something.

'Well…well we've been living separate lives for a long time. Probably for the last five years. It was probably over even before that.'

'So did you move out, or did she?'

Harvey hesitated before answering. 'Neither of us moved out. It seemed silly to go through the whole selling up and buying other places, so we came to an arrangement where we both still live in the same house, but go our separate ways. It's worked out okay for both of us.' He looked at Donna. 'You look worried.'

'I suppose I am. I'm surprised you didn't tell me you were still living together.'

'Only for convenience. Hon, you don't need to worry.' He looked deep into her eyes, and stroked her hair. 'Truly, we're separated, in separate bedrooms, and it's been over for a long time.'

'What went wrong in your marriage?' asked Donna, mindful of Trudy's enquiry.

'Long story. Let's keep that for another time, hey?'

'Okay.' Donna hesitated, trying to ignore the uncomfortable feeling in her stomach. 'Ready for berries and ice cream?'

'Sounds great. And just before you go and get that…'

He took her in his arms, then kissed her. She loved the way he kissed.

'You're still looking concerned,' he said. 'Honestly, it's okay. You've got nothing to worry about. I promise you.'

'Okay.'

She made her way into the kitchen, and got the mixed berries out of the fridge. Earlier in the day she'd soaked them in port. She placed two small neat scoops of ice cream in each bowl, and topped that with the berries.

She decided to put aside any concerns over what Harvey had told her. Maybe it was quite kosher. She knew couples sometimes had this kind of workable arrangement. It certainly wasn't like that with Martin. As soon as he told her about Trisha he moved out. Couldn't wait to be with her. She sighed. Time to put that behind her and move on.

She took the desserts into the dining room and sat down. Harvey smiled at her. He had a lovely smile. She felt herself melting. She was probably being silly to react. Before long they'd slipped back into a comfortable banter.

'Want some coffee and port?' she asked as the berries were devoured.

'Sounds good.'

'Let's move back into the lounge room and have them there?' Donna asked.

'Sure.'

Donna poured the coffee and took it into the lounge, where Harvey was already comfortably sitting on the couch. He had a twinkle in his eye. She loved that twinkle. She knew what it signalled.

She set the coffee on the table, and sensuously slipped off her dress, with a seductive strip-tease. My God, she thought, who would ever have imagined I'd have been behaving like this. She smiled as she watched Harvey's face. His eyes widened as she stripped down to her new black lingerie.

'Wow. You look stunning.'

He reached out for her, and kissed her again.

They didn't get to finish their coffee, and they didn't get to the bedroom.

'Do we still call this the "bed thing"?' she joked.

This was the first time she'd made love on these couches, but she decided it would not be the last time. Donna smiled to herself. She felt very contented as she lay in his arms, the earlier conversation now forgotten.

Chapter 7

'Can't wait to hear the next exciting instalment.' Nina moved in closer, facing Donna.

Donna smiled at her young friend, who was obviously vicariously enjoying watching how things were progressing.

'Well, things have been going well. I'm enjoying Harvey's company a lot.'

'And the sex,' Nina chimed in.

Donna laughed. 'I never expected to say this, but yes, the sex is sensational. And I like his mind too. He's very intelligent, and we can talk about anything from trivia to finding solutions for the problems of the world.'

'You're looking positively vitalised by the man,' said Halle. 'I haven't seen that look on your face before, ever.'

'I'm just trying to take it for whatever it is at the moment, don't know if we'll go walking off into the sunset together. I barely know him yet.' She paused. 'I get scared sometimes; this is all so new to me. But he's fun, and we do get on well.'

'We'll have to get to meet him. Why don't you ask him to my cocktail party?' asked Halle.

'Well, he's not usually here on the weekends. He goes back to Sydney.'

'So? The party's not on for another three weeks. Any reason he couldn't stay back in Melbourne for it?'

'Probably not. I suppose he's got plenty of time to re-arrange anything else he might have on. I'll ask him. I'd like you guys to meet him.' She was quiet for a moment. 'It would be good to get your reactions to him.'

'Why does he go back to Sydney on the weekends?' asked Paula.

'I don't know. Probably because it's home. He's down here during the week because work is based down here.' Donna sat back, then after a moment asked, 'So what's been happening with the rest of you?'

'Well, I had dinner with Tilly this week. She has an idea for a play that could be good,' said Halle, hesitantly.

Tilly was Halle's daughter, who fancied herself as a screenwriter, but had never come up with the goods. No-one answered.

Halle sighed. 'Yes, I know, you've heard it all before. You don't believe it's going to happen, do you?'

'Probably not. You know we don't think it's a good idea for you to keep supporting her while she sits on her bum all day. You work like a dog, and she sits up there in the hills pretending to be a screenwriter,' snapped Nina. 'She's only twelve years younger than me, but she's never done anything but sponge off you.'

'Yeah. I know you're right, but...' Halle sighed again, and sat without saying any more for a moment. Then, 'Maybe one day she'll prove herself. At least, that's what I'm hoping for.'

'As long as you don't hold your breath while you wait,' retorted Nina. 'I know it's not easy choosing to be in the arts. I have times when I'm waiting for the next commission, and sometimes my paintings don't sell for a while. But at least I'm working. I don't sit around doing nothing, just waiting for inspiration to descend on me. I've had to be disciplined and work at it. Tilly has never had the commitment. It's more the idea of being a screenwriter that she likes.'

'Yeah, I know.'

'Halle's hoping it'll happen one day, though' offered Donna, seeing her friend's discomfort.

'Not much evidence of that so far,' Nina replied.

Halle sat back with a long sigh; she'd closed down. Donna felt how painful it must be for her to accept that her daughter was exploiting her good nature. She let things stay quiet for a moment, in case Halle wanted to say more, but she stayed silent.

'Did you realise it's coming up for the anniversary of Gina's death?' Donna asked after a while.

A couple of the women nodded.

Nina said, 'Christ, a year already? I can't believe it.'

'I thought it might be good for us to go to the cemetery together. Anyone interested in doing that?'

'Yes, I'm in,' said Halle.

The others indicated that they'd like to go, too.

'So it falls two weeks from tomorrow. What time do you want to make it?'

There was conversation back and forth, until they settled on two o'clock. They agreed to all meet at Trudy's, and leave from there.

A silence fell on the group.

'I still can't believe she's gone. Sometimes I go to pick up the phone and call her,' said Halle.

Donna agreed, and told them how she still sometimes walked into Rick's expecting to see her at the table. 'Do you remember how she'd always have us in stitches. She was a fun woman with such a big heart.'

'She never did come to terms with turning fifty, did she?' added Halle. 'But the rest of us could see that she had still so much to live for.'

'We sure had some great times together,' said Nina.

The women became silent for a couple of minutes, each of them seemingly focussed on the memories of their friend. Halle wiped away a tear, then lifted her glass. 'I miss you heaps, Gina. Hope you can hear me. Let's drink to our wonderful Gina, the life of every party.'

They all drank to her.

'It reminds me of how lucky I've been, said Halle. 'Nearly six years now since my surgery. That could easily have happened to me, too. Not everyone gets through breast cancer as well as I have.'

'Well, you're here, thank God,' said Trudy.

'Yeah. And loving life.'

'So what's been happening in that life of yours? We haven't heard much about it for a while,' asked Paula.

'That's because not much has been happening.' She paused. 'Although I do have a date next Saturday night.'

'Man or woman?' asked Nina.

'A woman.'

'Where did you meet her? What's she like?' Trudy asked.

'She's a CFO with one of the banks. A real high-powered exec.' She hesitated. 'Maybe even too much so for me. But I find her attractive. I met her at a work do. She approached me, which is probably a good sign. Anyway, we'll see.'

The group had seen Halle's struggles with her sexual identity over the years. They'd been there through the trauma of her leaving her twenty-year marriage when she'd unexpectedly fallen in love with Frida, one of her work colleagues. Together the women in the group had been through the ups and downs of that relationship, which ended five years ago. Since then they'd watched Halle drift from relationship to relationship.

'So we'll wait and see,' said Nina.

'Yeah, to be continued. I wish I could make up my mind. But I'm sick of going from one person to another. I'd like a proper relationship. Just don't know whether I want to be with a man or a woman.'

'It's just that you haven't met the right one. I'm sure when he or she comes into your life you'll stop asking yourself the question. You'll know,' said Trudy.

'I hope you're right. I'll keep you posted, of course. Thank God for all of you. You've kept me afloat through my bits of madness.'

'I need some desserts now,' said Paula. 'My comfort food.'

'Feeling low?' asked Donna.

'A bit flat. I'm still getting my head around this retirement stage of life.'

'Yes, I know what you mean,' said Trudy. 'I'm finding in the year since I sold the Home and Garden shops I'm feeling quite lost. It's hard moving from being in business to having all that time on your hands.'

'Well, I thought my days were going to be full of the things I've always wanted to do, but now I'm feeling like I haven't got the motivation to try any of them,' said Paula.

'It's only been a short while. What is it, six months? It's a big adjustment from having all that structure around your nine to five life,' Donna replied.

'Yes, it could be that. Sometimes I wonder if it's because I'm missing Fran more now that I've got all this leisure time. I always expected that we'd be able to spend more time together once I retired.'

The women were silent, in their silence acknowledging Paula's pain. Finally, Donna responded,

'Yeah. It must be really difficult. How long is it now? Two years?'

'Yes. Two years next week.'

'Anniversaries are always hard,' said Trudy

'I always thought you didn't give yourself the chance to properly grieve after she died. I remember you went straight back to work, and you were crazy busy,' said Donna.

Paula didn't reply immediately. Then she answered, 'Perhaps you're right. It's not that I didn't feel raw, but I kept pushing myself to work and to keep filling my time. Now that I'm not busy any more...' She wiped away the tears that had started to roll down her cheeks, and immediately replaced them with a stoic smile.

'Hey, Paula. You don't need to do that with us,' said Trudy.

'Do what?' Paula looked genuinely puzzled.

'You don't need to go into strong woman mode. For your own sake you need to be able to let go. We know you're strong. But having a daughter killed in a car accident is a gut-wrenching trauma, and you've been too brave. You're going to keep having those bouts of depression if you keep holding on so hard.'

'I feel like it's not normal after all this time.'

'You've got to let yourself feel what you feel. There's no way through it but through it,' Halle responded.

Paula didn't answer immediately, but sat reflecting what the others had been saying. Finally she acknowledged, 'I think you're right. No, actually I know you're right. It's just so damn hard.'

'Yes it is. It's probably the worst thing that you could experience,' said Halle. 'All we can do is remind you that we're here for you. We can't make it go away, but talk to us, cry with us…whatever you need to do.'

'Thanks.' The tears were flowing again, but this time Paula did not try to stop them.

Donna knew how inconsolable she would be if anything had happened to Becky or Luke. She shuddered, and at that moment had even greater empathy for her friend's pain.

The women sat quietly, silently supporting Paula in the deep ache that they knew she was feeling.

Chapter 8

It was just before two, and the women had all arrived at Trudy's. They made their way out to her car, then drove to the cemetery, which was just a few minutes away. They walked to Gina's grave in silence. They'd brought flowers to place there, and had planned for each of them to choose a reading or speak some personal words to their friend.

'I don't want to be too sombre about it,' Nina had declared. 'Not because I'm not sad as all hell that she's gone, but I feel I want to say something that celebrates her life.'

'Yes, there was a lot to celebrate,' Halle had answered.

The women stood quietly around their friend's grave for a few minutes.

'So who's going to go first?' asked Paula.

Donna answered, 'I don't mind starting.' Then she continued, 'Gina darling, I'm so grateful for the times we shared together, and I'll never forget what you brought into my life. I chose a piece from Kahlil Gibran. I know you loved him.'

She paused for a moment, then read the words that spoke of how joy and sorrow were inseparable. Her eyes misty, Donna added, 'So my sorrow at the loss of you reflects the joy that you brought into my life. Just keep those angels laughing.' She took a yellow rose from the bunch they'd brought and placed it on the grave. 'We know these were your favourite flowers, so this is just a reminder of the wonderful part you played in our lives.'

One by one the women spoke, each placing a rose on their friend's grave, then they stood without speaking for a couple of minutes.

Donna looked around the group. Suddenly her eyes rested on Paula, who was standing, frozen, staring ahead of her. She realised with a jolt what this must be evoking in their friend. She'd forgotten that Fran was also buried in this cemetery. Looking at Trudy, she saw that she'd noticed too.

'Are you okay, Paula?' Donna asked.

'No, I feel terrible.'

'Would…would you like to go to Fran's grave now, too?' asked Trudy.

'I thought about it, but I don't know if I can bear it. Ted has offered to come here with me…but…but it hasn't felt right. Well, more honestly, I know it's that I haven't felt ready.' She hesitated for a moment, brushing aside a tear. 'It's felt too hard. I'm ashamed to admit this, but I haven't been here since the funeral. It's too painful, and I'm afraid I'll fall apart if I go.'

'We'll come with you, if you like. And if you do fall apart we'll be there to help you,' said Donna.

Paula was silent for a couple of minutes, then spoke haltingly. 'I'm…I'm not sure. I need to go, but I'm scared. I feel as if I'm barely holding together right now, and I'm afraid all my messy pieces will spill out.'

'That's what we're here for,' said Nina. 'We've all seen each other's messy pieces. Come on, let's go.'

She took Paula by the arm, and the five women walked together towards Fran's grave.

Donna looked a little worriedly at Paula. She hoped they'd be able to help her through this. She hated seeing her friend in so much pain. Surely there was something she could do to help her through it.

When they arrived at the graveside they gathered around Paula, who stood quietly. Without further prompting, she read the words on her daughter's tombstone. Then she crumbled, and a deluge of tears followed. She continued to sob for a long time, her face contorted with pain. At some moments it seemed that she had stopped, then the grief would pour out again. Sometimes her body looked like it would collapse, and one of the women held her; at other times it felt more appropriate to let her stand alone for a while.

Eventually the tears started to subside.

'Oh God, how I've needed that. I've just held on so tight, for far too long. But I thought a lot about what you all said, and I know I've needed to let it out.' She paused. 'I'm so grateful you're all here with me. I couldn't have done this without you. I've felt so guilty about not coming here, but I just didn't feel strong enough. Thanks for giving me that strength.' She smiled at them. 'I feel so unbearably sad, but I feel lighter, too.'

The women stood for a few minutes, talking to Paula and each other. After a while Trudy said, 'Okay, how about coming back to my place for a drink and something to eat?'

'I sure could do with it now. Let's go,' said Paula.

They walked back to the car and were soon immersed in conversation and occasional laughter.

~~

As they sat around at Trudy's, chatting over their drinks, Halle asked Donna, 'Did you ask Harvey to come to my cocktail party next week?'

'Yes, he's coming to the unveiling.'

'Unveiling?' Halle looked confused.

Donna laughed. 'The unveiling of the beau,' she replied.

'See you all there next week, then,' said Halle. 'Eight o'clock. Don't eat anything before you come. There's lots of finger food. I promise I won't send you home hungry. Or thirsty!'

The women started to say their goodbyes as they gradually left to go to their homes.

Donna walked over to Trudy's mantelpiece, which held several photos. There was one of their group. When had it been taken? Must have been four years ago. She felt sad as she gazed at Gina, sitting right in the middle, looking the picture of health, and with that beautiful, mischievous smile. *You left us too soon, my darling friend.* She was reminded of her regular message to herself: Carpe Diem.

Chapter 9

The hum of voices filled the room. Donna looked around and admired the impeccable décor. Halle certainly knew how to create a beautiful space, with soft tea lights scattered in different spots through the room, and flowers in varying shades of mauves and purples providing a wonderful splatter of colour. This was carried through to the surrounding terrace, and the garden below was also dotted with lights. The ambience she'd created was wonderful. And she hadn't been exaggerating when she'd promised there'd be plenty of good food to eat.

Donna smiled at the young waitress as she accepted the sushi that was offered. The food had just kept coming all night. So had the wine. She was starting to feel a little light-headed and giggly, and decided she'd switch to water soon. She didn't usually drink as much as she had tonight. Well, she was feeling a little nervous. After all, this was the first time she'd introduced Harvey to these friends who were so important to her. Up till that night it had always just been the two of them.

She had been chatting to one of Halle's business associates and his wife. She saw Harvey across the other side of the room, politely ended their tête-à-tête, and made her way over to him. He was busily engaged in conversation with Nina, Paula and Ted, and Trudy and Alan, and didn't look at her or interrupt his conversation as she quietly linked her arm through his, but gave her arm a silent squeeze. He was good at holding the floor, with his ready wit and charm. She wished she could be more like that. The Donna of the past used to be more at ease in a crowd. She sighed. That seemed like another lifetime ago.

She wondered what her friends felt about Harvey. And how he felt about them, too. She wanted them to like each other. But they seemed to be responding well to him. And he was always entertaining and charming. What was there not to like? Trudy winked at her and nodded. Her friend always had an uncanny ability to pick up on what she was thinking.

'Hon, would you like another drink?' Harvey's voice interrupted her thoughts.

'Nooooo thanks. No more bubbly.' She laughed. 'I've had more than enough. Perhaps some water if you're going over there.'

Harvey smiled and squeezed her hand. 'Back in a minute.'

As soon as he walked away Nina said, 'Good one, gal. He gets a tick from me. In fact, it's infused me with courage. I'm going to do the One Plus One thing tomorrow, I've decided.'

'That's great, Nina. Good move,' said Paula. 'And Donna, he seems okay. Good mind, and a lot of fun.'

Donna smiled. 'So you reckon the "unveiling" has been successful.'

'Yeah. Good pick.'

'What's a good pick?' Harvey was at her side, water in hand, smiling.

Donna laughed. 'Don't be cute. You know they're talking about you.'

Harvey had a look of mock surprise, then burst into laughter. 'Good. Glad I passed the test.' He handed her the glass, and announced, 'I decided to switch to water, too. Get ready for the drive home later.'

The music started up, and Harvey took her hand. 'Want to put your water down for a minute and dance?'

Donna was already swaying to the rhythm of the music provided by a three piece combo in the corner of the large room, and after taking a sip put her glass on a counter and followed Harvey into the middle of the room. They were the first to start dancing. She was a little self-conscious at first, but soon succumbed to the pleasure of the music and dancing to one of her favourite Beatles' songs.

'Another first, hey. We haven't danced together before, have we?' he asked.

'Mm. Feels wonderful.'

Harvey didn't answer, but looked into her eyes and drew her closer. She could feel his lips against her head, and his warm breath sent a wave of electricity through her body. Now she understood what people meant when they talked about feeling like a teenager again.

'This could get to be a habit, you know,' she whispered. 'I could get to like this.'

'I'll have to keep working on it, then.'

Donna felt an involuntary shudder move through her body.

'Are you okay?' he asked.

'Very okay, thank you.' Those surges of electricity. She hadn't expected to feel like that again. She laughed. 'Mm. What you do to me. I think you're a magician.'

'You won't believe what else I've got up my sleeve.'

She realised the music had stopped. She smiled at him. 'Had enough, or do you want to keep dancing to our own music?' she asked.

Harvey chuckled. 'I'm enjoying the excuse to hold you close.'

'You need an excuse?'

He kissed her lightly, then took her hand. 'Come on, before people start talking about us. Let's get back to your friends. Plenty of time for this later.'

They walked back to where the others were standing in one of the corners of the room.

'Hey there, Harvey. What have you done to our friend? She was here earlier in the evening, but you've brought this younger woman back with you,' laughed Nina.

'I just told him he was a magician,' Donna responded, a broad smile on her face. She felt good. She knew she was glowing. And the few kilos she'd dropped in the time since she'd met Harvey didn't hurt either.

'It's wonderful to see you looking so happy again,' said Halle, who had wandered over from the kitchen. Then she said to Harvey, 'She's been through a tough few years, and it's good to see her like this.'

Donna got the subliminal subtext of her friend's words. She was telling Harvey to look after her. Protective as always. But that's how they all were with each other.

~~

It was close to midnight, and the crowd was starting to dissipate. Donna and Trudy both made their way to the bathroom, before heading off home for the evening.

'So you like him, hey?' Donna asked.

'Yeah, I can see what you like about him. Only thing is…'

'What?'

'Look, it's probably nothing. I worry about his home arrangement. I asked him something about it, and it felt like he changed the subject quickly.'

'Well…he's just met you. His living arrangements mightn't be ideal, but I suppose it's the most practical thing for now. Maybe he didn't feel comfortable talking about it. Give him time. He's told me the situation, and I'm sure it's okay.'

'I hope so. Anyway, I want to get to know him better. How about the two of you coming over for dinner one night?'

'Love to. Give me a date and I'll check it out with him.'

'Okay. I'll give you a call tomorrow while he's still here and we can find a time that works.'

'Okay. Call me in the morning.'

'Talk to you tomorrow. And see you on Saturday at Rick's.'

Donna looked at her friend. Sometimes she wished she wouldn't ask those questions. They made her anxious. And besides, things were going so well with Harvey. She felt a surge of pleasure thinking about him. Sometimes Trudy worried too much.

Chapter 10

'That was a great party, Halle. You do it so beautifully. Puts me to shame. I wouldn't know where to start. Probably why I never do it,' Nina exclaimed. She laughed. 'Plus I'm too poor to be able to do anything like that. That's the life of a struggling artist, though. I suppose when I die all my work will sell for squillions, but it doesn't look like it's ever going to happen while I'm here to enjoy the spoils. Anyway, you excelled yourself.'

'Thanks. Glad you enjoyed it. And I know I'm lucky I can just phone people and organise stuff,' replied Halle. 'One of the perks of my work. But I'd love to have your talent, so…you know what they say about the grass being greener.'

'I'd wondered if you were going to invite that woman to your party that you spoke about at our last lunch. How's that going?' asked Paula.

'We had a great time. I thought about inviting Sophia - that's her name - but decided it was too early yet. We've only met a couple of times. Just taking things slowly. But I do like her. She's a lot of fun when you get her away from the work environment. Not as daunting as I thought.' She smiled. 'So…we'll see.'

Halle turned to Donna. 'And what about your man! Harvey seems nice. Fitted in so well, too. He's very easy to be around. And not hard to look at, either, by the way.'

Donna laughed. 'Yes, agree with all of the above. Can't believe it. I was remembering the other day about how apprehensive I felt when Becky suggested I try the internet. I got lucky, meeting Harvey so quickly.' She paused. 'I must admit I was nervous about you all meeting him. I'm glad you liked him. You did tell me you were going to screen him for me,' she added with a smile.

'So far so good,' said Halle. 'I'm looking forward to getting to know him better.'

'Have you done anything about putting a profile up?' Donna asked Nina. 'You'd said you were ready to go.'

'No, I was going to get onto that last Sunday, but Tony had a leave pass, so I spent the day with him and put One Plus One on hold.' She smiled wryly.

'Does that mean you've changed your mind?' Paula asked.

'No. I haven't changed my mind. I'll get onto it this weekend.'

'Hm,' said Trudy.

'What's the "hm" about?' asked Nina.

'Well, I'm just worried that Tony has charmed you again and distracted you from moving on. It's your life, and you'll do what you want, but you know we worry about you and what's best for you in the long run.'

'Yeah, I know what you're saying. And I am going to do it…tomorrow.'

No-one responded. Nina laughed. 'Truly, I know you don't believe me. But I'm onto it. I even started working on my profile. And yes, I did get waylaid, but nothing's changed. I still know I've got to make some big adjustments to my life.'

'Good. Glad to hear it,' said Trudy.

'And Donna,' Nina continued, 'I must admit that I'm encouraged by seeing Harvey and seeing it's not just dorks out there. It could actually be fun. So tomorrow's the day. It's only a minor detour; but I'm back on track. Anyway, moving right along…' she laughed.

Donna turned to Paula. 'How have you been since the cemetery?'

Paula didn't answer immediately, then responded, 'A bit up and down. Sometimes I just seem to suddenly start crying and I feel like I'm never going to be able to stop. But I'm glad you encouraged me to go to Fran's grave, even though it was so hard. It was a relief in a way.' She was quiet for a moment, then added, 'I know I've got to go through that. I just have to trust that it will get better over time. Well, that's what they say, isn't it? That time heals?'

'Yeah,' said Donna. 'I remember when I was going through that terrible time, I didn't believe that life could ever be good again. Sometimes it's hard to imagine anything could ever change, isn't it?'

Paula nodded. 'Thanks again, everyone. I don't know what I'd do without you.'

Lunch arrived at that moment, and the conversation drifted to how good everyone else's lunches looked.

'Why does that always happen?' laughed Halle. 'We take forever choosing what we want, but as soon as anyone else's food arrives I find my mouth watering for what they've got.'

Paula laughed. 'Well, you can have my rabbit food. Yours looks so much more interesting. I'm trying to lose some weight. In fact...I wanted to talk to you all about this...I'm wondering about going to speak to someone about lap band surgery.'

No-one answered immediately, then Nina exclaimed, 'Christ, woman, are you mad? You're nowhere near big enough to be considering that. In fact if you went to talk to someone about it they'd laugh you out of the office. I don't know what you see when you look at yourself in the mirror, but it's obviously not the same as others see.'

Paula blushed. 'That's because I choose my clothes carefully. Always trying to hide my weight.'

'Christ, Paula, that's crazy! We keep telling you you're not as big as you say you are. Sure, you may be a tiny bit overweight, but you're not obese. You've got a bloody distorted picture of yourself.' Nina was almost yelling, obviously feeling stirred up about what her friend was proposing. 'You need to see a psychologist, not a lap band surgeon. I keep telling you this is about your self-esteem. You thought you'd feel better when you had that Botox stuff done to your face, but how long did that last? And it would be the same with lap band surgery, even if some idiot did agree to do it...which they won't, by the way. Give it time and you'd be looking for the next dose of the magic "feel good about Paula" elixir.

Paula was quiet. She looked embarrassed by Nina's response. 'Phew,' she said. 'That was quite a serve. Ted had a reaction, too, when I talked to him about it. But I just keep looking at myself and seeing this…this blob. I keep remembering how skinny I used to be, and I actually feel ashamed sometimes about how I'm looking now.'

'Paula, you need to stop comparing your body now to your thirty year old body. Get real, it's never going to be like that again,' Nina continued.

Paula paused, then asked, 'You really don't think I'm ginormous?' She sounded incredulous, and gave an embarrassed laugh. 'You guys always give me something to mull over. Thing is, in the end I usually get to see you're right about most things. That's why I like to talk to you.'

Donna looked at Nina; she loved how direct and honest she was, even though it was sometimes confronting. She was so open and so uniquely herself. Even if Donna were to have a similar thought, she knew she had a tendency to soften the blow; she would carefully measure her words. Not Nina, though. 'No orange light,' Trudy had once said after a particularly strong outburst at one of their lunches. Mind you, she could be too outspoken sometimes. But that was Nina.

There was silence while they started eating. Donna glanced across at Paula, who was sitting opposite. She thought she looked relieved to have the distraction of food after her exchange with Nina.

The tension that had temporarily been stirred up by their discussion dissipated, and before long the women were enjoying their meal and talking lightheartedly again. The waitress arrived at their table soon after to collect their dishes and tell them what desserts were on for today.

'So Donna,' Halle asked during one of the lulls in conversation, 'how old are Harvey's kids?'

'Twenty one and seventeen.'

'Living with their mother, I suppose? Do they spend much time with Harvey?'

Donna paused for just a moment before replying, 'Well, actually…well, they're all still living in the family home. He's separated from his wife, they're living separate lives, but they decided it suited them both to stay in the house for now, rather than do the property settlement thing and sell up. And his younger son is doing HSC this year and it would have been hard to disrupt things for his sake.'

Halle didn't say anything immediately. Then she looked straight at Donna.

'And you're okay with that?'

'Yeah. It works for them both.'

'I wouldn't like it. I wouldn't feel okay about that at all. It's like he's got a foot in each camp, even if they do lead separate lives.' She paused. 'But I suppose if you're comfortable with it…'

'Well he's reassured me that it's a practical decision. I think it's all okay. And don't forget he's only there on weekends, anyway. He's here during the week. So I suppose seeing he's back there so little of the time it's not a bad arrangement.'

'Yeah…I suppose you're right,' replied Paula. 'Anyway, what's everyone having for sweets? After sacrificing for mains I wouldn't mind desserts.' After perusing the choices she added, 'Bummer, suppose I'd better be sensible and order a fruit platter. Anyone interested in sharing?'

'Sounds too healthy,' laughed Nina. 'I'm lusting after the chocolate soufflé.'

'Lemon tart for me,' said Halle. 'I don't know if you're going to get any takers, Paula.'

'I'll do the fruit platter with you,' Donna offered.

'Thanks, Donna. You've saved me from myself. I almost weakened when Nina talked about the soufflé. Now I can get back to feeling virtuous.'

The women placed their orders, then got engrossed in their conversation again.

The waitress was soon back with their desserts, and they continued with their lunch, enjoying the blend of good food interspersed with chatter.

'Okay, I'm going to need to break up the party soon,' Halle declared. 'I'm off to a late afternoon movie.'

'With...?' asked Nina.

'With Sophia.'

'Well, enjoy. Look forward to hearing about it next time.'

The others paid for their meal and started to prepare for their departure too.

The friends hugged and made their way out to their cars.

Chapter 11

It was Tuesday, Donna's afternoon off work. She fluffed up a large cushion and made herself comfortable on the couch. She was looking forward to watching the next episode of Secrets and Lies that she'd recorded. She turned the set on, and settled back, a bowl of pasta balanced on her lap. The introductory music to the show started up, and she gave a sigh of satisfaction. Life was good.

The phone rang. Damn. She thought about not answering it, but reached out to her side table and picked it up.

'Hello. Donna speaking.'

'Donna, this is Shelley.'

'Shelley?' Donna was puzzled. 'Sorry, who is this? Do I know you?'

'You bloody well should know me.' The woman sounded furious. Donna's mind was racing, trying to put the pieces together. She was silent, not knowing what to say.

'I'm ringing to tell you to fucking *stay away from Harvey!*'

Donna's heart starting pounding. What was this woman talking about? Then she felt a searing pain in her gut. It couldn't be.

'What...what are you talking about?' she asked.

'I'm talking about the text messages I've picked up between the two of you. And then I checked the phone bill. All those calls to you. Did you think I wouldn't find out? What the hell are you doing?' She was sobbing now. 'How...how can you do this? Are you comfortable with being a home wrecker?'

The pieces were starting to fit together, but Donna was struggling with the ugliness of the picture they were forming.

'I don't understand. I thought you were separated. And you had an agreement about living your own separate lives.'

Now Shelley was silent. It seemed she was also putting pieces together at her end of the phone. Now there was just the sound of her crying. Finally she replied. 'No, there's no agreement. No agreement at all.' Then after a few moments she asked, 'Is that what he told you? That we're separated?'

'Yes.' Donna felt sick. Sick for herself and sick for the woman at the other end of the phone. 'I'm so sorry. I had no idea. My understanding was that you were still living together for convenience, but separated. That that was what you'd both agreed to.'

Shelley didn't answer for a while. Then she said quietly, 'No. We never agreed to anything of the sort.' She started to cry again. 'Oh God, he's up to his old tricks again. What an idiot I've been. I believed him when he promised me it would never happen again. I should have known the bloody leopard would never change his spots.'

'You mean he's done this to you before?' For a moment the pain for her own sense of betrayal was overshadowed by the empathy she felt for his wife. 'I'm so sorry, Shelley. I would never have agreed to see Harvey if I'd known the truth. I had no idea.'

Shelley was still crying. 'He's so bloody convincing. I believed him, too. It's not your fault. At the moment I feel devastated. I just found his phone this morning before he left for Melbourne. I haven't said anything to him yet. I…I'm still in shock. Oh God…it's like a bad dream.' She was silent for a moment. 'I need to hang up now. I…would you mind if I rang you back in a couple of days? I need to know what you're going to do about this. I can't think clearly at the moment. I don't know what I'm going to do either. It's complicated. You know, the kids and everything…Our son's doing HSC…

'Sure. Yes, it's okay if you want to call me back. Shelley, I…' Her words trailed off. She didn't know what else to say. She needed to digest this.

She hung up the phone, and sat staring into space. It felt like emotional gravity had deserted her. As if she were floating unnaturally, and things were upside down. Crazy disequilibrium. The feeling of the nightmarish quality of life she'd never wanted to bump into again.

She sat for a long time, trying to make sense of what had just happened, feeling numbness but at the same time a burning pain. After a while she dialed Trudy's number.

'Trudy, can I come over for a while?'

'Of course. Are you okay?'

Donna didn't reply to her friend's question. 'I'll be over there in a few minutes. Have a drink poured for me.'

She got into her car. She was shaking. She hoped she was okay to drive, but it wasn't far to Trudy's and she turned the key in the ignition.

~~

Donna drew the curtains and poured herself another drink. She'd stopped shaking now. She looked at the clock. Six thirty. Harvey was due in another fifteen minutes. She'd managed to calm down a little after talking to Trudy. But she still had to confront him now. Or maybe he just wouldn't turn up. Maybe Shelley had paid out on him and he would just not show.

Harvey had bought tickets for them to go to a concert tonight to see Il Divo. Fuck the tickets. She hoped they cost him a bundle. She felt so foolish now. How could she have been so naïve? How could she have believed him? But then she also argued with herself that he was very plausible. Why would she not believe him? And as Trudy had pointed out to her, she wasn't the only one who'd been duped; the girls had all given him the seal of approval too.

He'd probably be late again. She found herself on the one hand wanting to delay the necessary confrontation, and on the other hand

65

willing the time to pass quickly so she could get this whole sorry, sordid mess out of the way. She'd had some fairly grisly fantasies during the afternoon about what she'd like to do to the bastard. Quite unlike her. Then another part of her had the totally irrational fantasy that he'd have some explanation that would just make this whole thing go away. Just some sort of misunderstanding. But of course she knew this was crazy make-believe.

The doorbell interrupted her thoughts. She took a deep breath to steady herself before going to the door to answer it.

'Hi gorgeous.'

She stared at him, amazed. He was behaving as if everything was okay. He obviously hadn't spoken to Shelley. She didn't answer him, but looked straight at him with a cold, stony gaze.

'Are you okay? What's up?' he asked. He looked perplexed.

'Come in.'

He tried to hug her, but met with a shield of steel.

'What's wrong, Hon?' He looked at her, confused, but made his way to the couch without another word. The two of them sat without saying anything for a couple of minutes, then Donna said in a voice that was so calm she amazed herself.

'I had a call from Shelley today.'

Harvey didn't respond immediately. His face had drained of colour. Then he asked, 'She called you?'

'Uh-huh.' She didn't want to make it easy for him. She sat in silence, wanting him to squirm, waiting for him to speak.

'What did she say?'

'Well, for starters, she made it quite clear that what you've been telling me was bullshit.' She felt surprisingly powerful now. She enjoyed seeing him look uncomfortable.

'What do you mean?'

'Harvey, no more pretense, please. She read our text messages. She was very distressed. She told me that it was a complete surprise to hear from me that you were supposed to be separated. And she also told me that it's not the first time you've cheated on her. It seems she had given you the benefit of the doubt until she discovered about us.'

She sat watching him. He wasn't answering. So what was he going to do now? Come up with an excuse? Apologise? She was determined to wait for him to talk. She wanted to hear if he was going to try to wriggle out of this.

His face, previously drained of colour, was now flushed. After several minutes he looked at her and asked, 'So what do you want me to say?'

'What do *I* want you to say? Christ, Harvey, I want to hear from you what *you* want to say. I want to know how you could do this. How you could lead me down this path, how you could deceive me like that.'

Harvey's demeanour had shifted to one of defiance. 'Come on, Donna. We're not children. Things just happen sometimes. You meet someone, you like them. I like you a lot. I wanted to see how things developed. Things haven't been great at home for a long time, as far as I was concerned. I didn't know if I wanted to stay. That's why I told you Shelley and I were separated.'

God, had he been taking lessons from Martin? "Things just happen"? History re-run. She wasn't going to let another man tell her that. 'No, Harvey. Don't give me shit about things just happening. You deliberately deceived me. You lied to me; you put your profile up on One Plus One, and you pretended you were available. And I let myself get involved because I believed your lies.'

He didn't answer immediately. Finally he said, 'Okay, so I'm not perfect. You're right.' He was quiet now. For a moment he looked uncharacteristically lost for words. Donna sat without talking. Let the rat struggle.

'So what do you want to do now?' he asked.

'What I want now is for you to get the hell out of my house and never contact me again. I can't believe you could do this. Not to Shelley, and not to me.'

'Okay. I'm going.' He looked straight at her and said, 'Pity. I enjoyed being with you.' He got up, picked up his jacket and started to walk towards the door. 'If you change your mind you know where to contact me. We could just enjoy it for what it is. Not every relationship has to be "exclusive". We're good together. Think about it.'

Donna looked at him with disbelief. 'Are you for real? Get the hell out of here. I never want to talk to you again.'

She walked ahead of him to the door. 'And I hope you don't do this to any other woman who is genuinely looking for a relationship.'

Harvey lingered momentarily at the front door, looking as if he was going to say something else. Then he turned on his heels and walked away.

Donna walked back into the lounge room, fell onto the couch and started sobbing. She was glad she'd not cried while Harvey was there. She didn't want to give him that power. Her tears were a mixture of hurt and rage. How could someone be so unlike they seemed?

She knew she needed to hang onto the anger. That was how she'd get over this. And she told herself she would never let anyone deceive her like this again.

Chapter 12

Donna looked at herself in the mirror. Her eyes were red-rimmed and swollen. She'd cried last night until she thought there couldn't possibly be any tears left. But this morning when she woke up after what felt like a few minutes sleep she'd started to cry all over again. How could he do that to her? She remembered how he'd reassured her that she didn't need to worry about his living arrangements. How he'd urged her to stop worrying, and lied, with that fucking falsely genuine look on his face.

This morning, though, she was crying tears of rage. How could the bastard live with himself? And what now? Was he going to do the same to other women?

She reprimanded herself: how could she have been so stupid? But then she remembered how believable he'd seemed. He'd managed to sell himself effectively. *Arsehole! Bloody sociopath!* She paused, and went into the kitchen to make herself a coffee. Her face was burning with emotion. And her stomach was aching. Suddenly, before she had time to check in with her rational mind, she picked up the coffee cup and threw it against the wall. God that felt good. But a moment later, her sanity restored, she looked with amazement at the smashed pieces scattered on the bench and the floor. Damn, that had been one of her favourites.

She sat down at her computer, planning a verbal barrage in the imaginings of her mind. For the next half hour she wrote, a tidal wave of emotions spilling out in her words, as she told Harvey exactly what she thought of him; she didn't hold back on any of her hurt or her fury. For a while, with each sentence, her rage increased. But finally, it felt like she had spilled out enough venom, and she felt strangely liberated. She read what she had written. Then read it again. By the time she'd gone over her words three times she felt surprisingly calm. With a final glance, she took a deep breath and pressed the "delete" button. She didn't want to give him the satisfaction of a response. And besides, the writing had been good for her. She didn't need to send it now.

As she swept up the shards of crockery she felt a new kind of power she'd never known. Let Harvey swim in his own sea of pathetic muck. She felt lucky to be out of it. Life was a hell of a lot more than her interlude with Harvey, and she'd be damned if she was going to let him bring her down.

~~

A couple of weeks had passed, and each day Donna felt better. She was actually starting to feel a return to the Donna of her past. And yet not the same Donna. Somehow her experience with Harvey had summoned a new strength. And now she sometimes even felt elation, and the emergence of an inner freedom. Well, "they"…those wise mysterious unidentified people out there who seemed to know it all…did talk about pain and gain. She gave a sigh of satisfaction, glancing at the clock. It was their Saturday lunch, and Trudy was picking her up to go to Rick's. She heard the horn toot, collected her jacket and made her way out to the car.

She and Trudy were the first of the group to arrive. They were surprised to see Rick out front of house today. Although he'd sometimes come out briefly to say hello he was usually back in the kitchen.

'Hi, good to see you again.' He led them to their table in the corner.

'How come we've got you out here today, Rick?' Donna said.

'We've got a new chef,' Rick responded. 'Used to be at Chez Pierre. He started here a couple of weeks ago and he's fantastic.' He laughed. 'They're not needing me back there as much now. Looks like I might have almost made myself redundant.' He seated them, then added, 'I'll be interested to hear whether you like our new menu. Hope you enjoy your lunch.'

Donna smiled at their host. 'I'm sure we will. If you're confident about your new chef I doubt we're going to be disappointed.'

'Hi guys.' Nina's voice interrupted their conversation.

Paula and Halle approached at the same time, and they were soon all seated.

'We've got a new chef and new menu today,' Donna informed the latecomers.

'Hm. Hope all my faves haven't been dumped,' Nina responded.

The women were quiet for a while, reading with interest the new offerings.

'Yum, the goat looks wonderful,' said Halle.

'I'm going for the scallops,' Donna decided. 'My mouth's watering already.'

The general consensus about the new menu was positive, and each of them made their choice.

'Okay, now that we've got that out of the way…what's been happening since last month?' asked Paula.

'Well, girls. I did it,' announced Nina. 'You didn't believe me, but I'm up and running on One Plus One. And having a ball. I've been out with four guys already.'

'I'm pleased you've taken the plunge. Any you're interested in?' asked Halle.

'A couple of potentials.' She laughed, then added, 'Still "auditioning" the contenders.'

'Have you told Tony what you're doing?' asked Trudy.

'Yeah, you bet. He's not a happy chappy about it. He actually got pissed off. Can you believe it, he's pissed off with *me* because I'm seeing other guys. Who knows, it may make him keener.'

'So are you going to keep seeing him?' asked Donna.

Nina hesitated. 'Yes, I will for now. I know I need to end it but I'm not ready yet. I'm still finding it hard to walk away.'

'Yeah, it is hard. But you're not giving yourself a chance to move on if you've got one foot in and one foot out,' said Halle. 'You're playing it safe. You need to finish it with Tony.'

Nina sighed, then snapped, 'Cut me some slack, will you. I'm taking it a step at a time. I'll probably stop seeing Tony if I meet someone else I like.' She looked flushed and annoyed. Then after a moment she added, 'I know you're probably right, and I'll get there. It's just going to take me time.'

'Yeah, I get that. But just remember that biological clock we talked about. It doesn't stop ticking,' said Trudy.

Nina nodded, then drifted away into her own thoughts. She looked stirred up. After a couple of minutes she said, 'Can you let it go now? I've heard you, but I don't want to talk about it any more now.'

'Okay,' Halle said.' Then she turned to Donna. 'So tell us about how things are going with your gorgeous guy.'

'They're not. We're finished. My "gorgeous guy" turned out to be a real arsehole,' Donna responded.

'What? What the hell happened? You were getting on so well. I can't believe it. God, I thought I was going to have to start saving for a wedding present,' said Halle.

'No wedding bells, I assure you. The bastard is still very much married. The stuff about being separated was bullshit. I had a call from his wife a couple of weeks ago. She was distraught. She knew nothing of their supposed "separation". He was lying to me.'

'My God, Donna, are you okay? That's awful! You must be devastated,' said Halle.

'I'm surprisingly okay. I'm more angry than anything. It threw me around at first, but I bounced back pretty quickly; I amazed myself, to tell you the truth. I decided I'm not going to let him drag me down. The bastard isn't worth it.'

Trudy smiled fondly at her friend. Donna looked back at her; she knew that Trudy had initially been anxious that she'd fall in a heap. In the first couple of days after the situation with Harvey had erupted, Trudy had kept phoning her to check if she was alright. Probably worried she was suicidal again. Finally Donna had reassured her, 'Trudy, I know you're concerned I'm going to do the same as I did before. Please don't worry, it's just not going to happen. I'm okay. I'm more furious than anything else. I'm not going to try and kill myself. I'm feeling much more like killing him. So stop worrying. I'm alright.'

It felt good for Donna to recognise how much more resilient she was. She was never going to fall apart the way she had when Martin had left home.

'So what now?' asked Paula. 'Are you going to go back on the internet? Or is that it?'

'Yes, I will. I just need a while to re-group, then I'll put my profile up again.'

'Good on you,' said Halle.

Donna smiled. 'You can't keep a good girl down,' she said.

Rick appeared at their table as they were talking. 'Just thought you might all enjoy some port. Any takers?'

'Lovely. Thanks for that, Rick,' said Donna.

The others chorused their appreciation.

'Do you want to join us?' asked Nina.

'I'd love to, but it just got busy out back. Maybe another time. By the way, how did you find the food?'

'Three hats. Beautiful. Just what we've come to expect here, though,' said Nina, smiling at him.

'Sounds like that means you'll be back,' laughed Rick.

'You bet. You know we can't stay away,' replied Nina.

'Glad to hear it. You'll be seeing some more changes soon. Going to be doing a makeover here. And probably changing the name to Ricardo's. Anyway, I must go. See you soon, enjoy your port.'

They sipped as they continued their chatter. Then Donna turned to Halle, asking, 'So what's happening with you, Halle? Any new developments with Sophia?'

73

'Actually things are chugging along well.' Halle was blushing, Donna noticed. 'I like her a lot. In fact I...I actually think I'm falling in love with her. We get along so well. I can't believe it.' She smiled. 'You told me I'd stop trying to work out if I wanted to be with a man or a woman when the right one came along. I feel I might have met that right one. It's amazing.'

'That's terrific. When can we meet her?' asked Nina.

'I've been wondering about that. I thought I might make a dinner and you guys can come along and get to know her. How about we pencil in a night?'

'Love to. That'd be great,' said Nina.

They took out their diaries, and arranged a night a couple of weeks later.

'I'll check with Sophia and confirm in the next couple of days.'

'Great. Okay, I need to go,' said Paula, starting to leave the table. Nina was still sitting.

'Are you coming, Nina?' asked Donna.

Nina didn't immediately respond, but then answered, 'No, I'm going to just sit here for a while and finish my drink. And I've got a couple of calls to make. See you all at Halle's in a couple of weeks.'

Donna glanced at their friend, but merely threw her a kiss, as she followed the others out of the restaurant.

Chapter 13

'How are you doing?' Trudy asked. She'd called Donna that morning, saying she felt like a catch up. Now they sat in Trudy's kitchen, drinking their second cup of coffee.

'Surprisingly okay. It's not that I'm not upset. And I'm still very angry. But I'm actually glad I got that call from his wife. The Harvey I thought I'd met wasn't the man he turned out to be. I feel so sorry for Shelley. She called me up last week to check if things were over between us now. She sounded very distressed. But she's still in there with him, and I'm lucky to be out of it. So I've moved on pretty well, considering.' She smiled. 'I even got around to putting my profile back on One Plus One, and I've had a few responses already.'

'What are they like?' Trudy looked worried.

'Don't worry, Trude. I'll be cautious. I've learned my lesson. I'll be asking the right questions from the get-go from now on.'

'Good. I don't want to see any more Harveys hanging around my friend.'

'Me either. I'll be on red alert this time.'

'So tell me about these lucky new guys. Have you met any of them yet?'

'I had coffee with one yesterday; his name was Gary. A bit old in his ways, even though we're the same age, and there was no spark at all.' She laughed. 'I'd have felt like I was going out with my Uncle Bill. Similar type.'

'Did you tell him?'

'Yes. Well I didn't tell him he reminded me of Uncle Bill, but I told him I didn't see us as suited. He didn't like hearing that. Went from being pleasantly boring to aggro. Wanted to know why I thought we weren't a match. I tried to tell him as best I could, but sometimes it's hard to define. Said he'd be in touch with me again. Not sure why, 'cause I did tell him there wasn't much point.'

Deep in thought, Trudy didn't respond immediately.

'What are you thinking?' said Donna.

'I don't know why, but I keep getting this feeling you'll hear from Harvey again.'

'What makes you say that? I bloody hope not. I told the lying bastard I never want to talk to him again.'

Trudy was silent.

'What's going through that mind of yours now?' asked Donna.

'Well…to tell you the truth I went off on a tangent. I was remembering my affair with Pete all those years ago. I don't know now how I could have gotten involved with him when I look back. But at least there was no pretending that it was anything other than what it was. Not like Harvey. Pete knew I was married, and I knew he was. Neither of us had any intention of leaving our partners.' She paused. 'That was when I was drinking a lot, remember? Can you believe it now? I had a big problem back then, though I didn't want to admit it at the time.'

'Yeah. It seems like forever ago, doesn't it? What was it, twenty years?'

'Yes, it would be. I was struggling, trying to come to terms with not being able to have kids. I wanted them so badly. It tore me apart. I was all over the shop, and acting out. Remember I went into therapy then? It took me a while to understand that my unhappiness had nothing to do with my marriage, that it was about me. And about grief. God, I nearly wrecked a good relationship. Thank goodness Alan and I were able to patch things up.' She stared into space, obviously caught up in the past. Then she said, 'It makes it easier for me to understand Nina. She's going through similar things to what I was then.'

'Yes, she knows time is running out. But she's also got her fears about fully committing to a relationship. In a way it's easier to be with Tony because he can only ever be part time. She's so scared of losing her freedom if she hooks up with someone who's actually available.'

'Yes, but at least she knows it and acknowledges it in her wiser moments.' Trudy was pensive. 'I hope she goes to see somebody to work through it all, or that someone will just catch her unawares and she'll find herself falling crazy in love before she knows it.'

'Hm. That would be good, wouldn't it?'

'Yep. Want all my friends to live happily ever after. That's not asking for too much, is it?' laughed Trudy.

'Hm, maybe just a smidge.'

'I'm a bit of a Pollyanna. By the way, what did you think of Sophia?' asked Trudy.

'I liked her very much. She's perfect for Halle. She comes across as tough at first, but she's a softie.'

'Yes. And funny.'

Donna glanced at her watch. 'Better go. I've got the kids coming for dinner tonight, and I promised I'd cook them a proper meal. I haven't done a lot of that for a while. One of the pluses coming out of my relationship with Harvey. I found I was enjoying cooking for someone else again.'

'The old silver lining thing,' smiled Trudy. 'Okay, enjoy cooking, and enjoy your family. See you next week at Rick's. But call me and let me know how you go with your guys. I'm living vicariously through you seeing I'm a good gal these days,' she laughed.

Donna hugged her friend, and walked to her car. She was soon focused on her shopping list and what to prepare for her family tonight. She'd seen a new Donna Hay recipe she thought she'd like to try. Chicken and haloumi with honey and lemon zest. Sounded simple and delicious. She found herself humming a song that had been playing in the background while she'd been with Trudy. She headed towards the shops.

~~

Donna was carrying the shopping inside, and heard the phone ring. It would have to go to message bank. She put the parcels down, and refrigerated the things that needed to be kept cold. She'd just have a cup of tea before she got down to preparing dinner. She settled down with the hot drink, and reached for the phone to check her messages. There were two. The first was from Becky, just wanting to check what time they were expected for dinner.

She went to the second message. Her body froze. It was from Harvey! Bloody hell, was Trudy clairvoyant? Smooth as silk, he was. Almost as if there was every reason in the world to be calling her. Just wondering how she was, and wondering if they might catch up "just for a drink and a chat". Donna glared at the phone, as if it were Harvey standing there. Was he insane? It seemed as if he was oblivious to her reaction when they'd last talked. She was shaking as she walked away from the phone. Tea just wouldn't do it now. She walked over to the wine rack, took the first bottle she could find and quickly poured herself a drink. What part of "I don't want to ever talk to you again" did that fucking idiot not understand?

She phoned Trudy. 'You must have had a premonition. I just had a message from Harvey wanting to catch up!'

'What are you going to do?'

'I'm not sure. Why doesn't he get it? I spelled it out clearly enough. Probably just doesn't give a damn what I want. I wish there was some way I could be certain he'll never call again.' Donna sat in silence. Then she said quietly, 'I don't want to hear his voice again.' She thought for a while longer, then added, 'I'll send him a text message telling him *again* not to contact me. And that if he does I'll have to do something more drastic. Hopefully he'll get the message this time and stop bothering me.'

Trudy didn't answer immediately, then asked softly, 'Are you okay now? Let me know if there's anything I can do for you…any time.'

'Thanks Trude. We'll talk soon. Bye.'

Donna hung up the phone, then picked up her mobile. She typed in her text message, saying clearly and firmly what she wanted to say. As she pressed the send button she wondered vaguely if Shelley would find her message. She felt very sorry for her.

She wiped away a stubborn tear. It was time to start getting dinner ready. They'd all be here in a couple of hours, and she looked forward to the chorus of voices that would soon fill her home.

Chapter 14

Donna walked into her house, parcels in each hand. She was excited to get inside and unpack. She'd been on a spending spree with Trudy. That new wardrobe of clothes she'd been promising herself. The old plum dress was looking much too tired. It was probably ten years old.

And her retail therapy had been a welcome treat, though she probably wouldn't have succumbed to the temptation of those last couple of outfits if not for her friend's encouragement. Not that she needed too much coaxing, if she was honest with herself.

She was looking forward to her own little private fashion parade now, as she took the clothes out of their bags. One by one, she slipped into her new outfits. She had to admit that one of the positive outcomes from her time with Harvey was that she didn't look too bad. More trim and toned. She smiled to herself. Something good that came out of the whole sorry mess.

The little black dress she pulled over her hips now hugged her body neatly. She let herself enjoy the vision that stared back at her from the mirror. Then she slid out of that, and into the zebra-striped pants. She'd hesitated when she tried them on in the store. Did sixty-year-old women wear zebra-striped pants?

'Of course you can wear them,' Trudy had assured her.

And she had to admit she looked okay. Maybe even pretty damn good, especially teamed with the little black camisole and jacket that looked like they were made for her. She was pleased Trudy had pressed her to buy these things, even though at first it felt indulgent.

'No harm in a bit of indulgence,' Trudy had insisted. 'You're due for some self-nurturing.'

Donna was still enjoying how this outfit enhanced her shape when she heard the doorbell. It was too early for Becky and James and the kids, who were not due for another hour. They were going to call in on their way to Tullamarine, before heading off to Europe. She probably should have insisted she take them to the airport, but Becky wouldn't hear of it. They were coming over to say goodbye, and were leaving their car in her garage while they were away, she'd reminded Donna. 'And I've already booked a cab to pick us up from your place.'

She walked down the stairs, feeling lighthearted. She gave a satisfied sigh, and walked to the door.

At first she thought she was imagining. He couldn't have that much nerve. Did he have no self-respect? Harvey gave her an awkward grin, hesitantly holding out a bunch of roses.

'Hello.'

She didn't answer.

'Can I come in, just for a minute?'

'No you can't come in. You've got a bloody nerve showing up here.'

He stood and looked at her. 'I knew it was no good phoning you. You hung up on me a couple of times. And I wanted to talk to you. But it's difficult to speak to you standing out here.'

'I don't want to talk to you. What do I have to do to make you understand that?'

'I'll be quick. I wanted to tell you that I've left Shelley. I just don't love her. I can't keep up the pretense any more. So now I'm free I'd like to see you again.'

Donna stared back at him. 'No, Harvey. I do not want to see you again. And please...read – my - lips. I do not want to ever hear from you again. Stay! Away! From! Me!' Her voice rose with each word.

She gave him one more cold, angry look before she stepped back and slammed the door.

'Don't you dare slam the bloody door in my face, you bitch!' He was banging on the door.

Donna's heart was pounding.

'Don't think you can just piss me off like that, you hear? Open the fucking door.'

She didn't answer, but stood frozen on the spot for a while. She didn't know how long. Eventually, after banging on the door one more time and yelling, she heard his footsteps receding down her front path. She turned on her heels, and walked towards the phone, the adrenalin still pumping. She checked her contacts, and dialed the number.

'Morrissey and Clarkson, Denise speaking' said the voice at the other end of the phone.

'Could I please speak to Jonathan Clarkson,' Donna asked.

'Sorry, he's in Court at the moment.'

'Okay, could you ask him to call me when he gets back to the office.' She gave the receptionist her name and number, and hung up. She took a couple of deep breaths to steady herself, then walked into her lounge room.

God, what she'd do for a cigarette, she thought, then was immediately shocked that she'd considered that. It had been six years since she'd quit smoking, and after a moment she felt grateful there were not any lying around to let her act on her impulse.

She was shaky. She needed to get it together before the family arrived. She walked over to her CDs, leafed through them and found one by Josh Groban. She sat back in the cushions and closed her eyes, letting Josh's soothing voice do its magic.

The man must be mad. Completely brainless when it came to reading what another person wanted. Well, more realistically, he obviously didn't care what anyone else wanted. Fucking narcissist. Too bad she had to go to these lengths to get rid of him. She felt amazed now that she could ever have thought she cared for him. She shuddered, and felt a surge of revulsion pass through her body.

~~

Donna sat drinking a glass of one of her favourite reds, a Pinot Noir from the Yarra Valley. It had been good to see her family this afternoon. Somehow she'd managed to push her earlier emotions underground for a while.

Her grandchildren had been so excited about their first trip overseas. Maddy, the oldest, couldn't stop talking about Paris. And London.

'We're going to see the Eiffel Tower,' she'd announced. 'And Buckingham Palace.'

Donna had felt a warm glow as she looked at her oldest grandchild. God, it seemed like no time since Becky was that age. She suddenly felt a wave of sadness. How different things had been then. There was no way she ever expected her life to move away from that trajectory. Life was supposed to always stay the same. No surprises.

She thought about that now, almost laughing out loud. Well, surprises there certainly had been. Who would ever have imagined that she'd be slamming the door on her ex-paramour? That there'd be any such person? That wasn't written into the agenda. These were the years that she and Martin were supposed to be enjoying their grandchildren together. Travelling. All the things they'd been unable to do when they were younger and had always talked about doing "when the children left home". Well, the children had left home now. And here she was, a sixty year old woman, in her zebra-striped pants, having slammed that door, having phoned her solicitor to talk about taking out a restraining order on the man who had just a short while ago entranced her, won her over with his charm, but who now left her feeling nauseous. And here she was responding to an unknown sea of men sending their "hugs" and emails from her profile on the internet. Definitely not in the script.

And suddenly she found herself sobbing. Sobbing uncontrollably. Not because she wanted to be back with Martin. Or Harvey. God, no, not that. But sobbing about the grief of it all. The end of the way things were supposed to be. The dashing of her expectations about how life might have evolved. The end of the hopes and dreams that she'd carried with her as a secure given.

She cried for a long time. But eventually she stopped. She wiped her eyes, and from among the ashes of her grief some other ember burned ever so softly. It was hope, or something resembling hope. Because she knew that she was in a new phase of her life, and although she'd experienced her share of disappointments a new sense of her future was emerging. She found herself wondering what was around the next corner, and even looking forward to the unexpected.

She took a couple of deep breaths, then opened her MacAir and went to check her emails.

Chapter 15

Donna looked at the email again in amazement. Some people just didn't have a clue, she decided, as she read the words from Gary, her "Uncle Bill" suitor, again.

> *Donna,*
> *We had an enjoyable conversation over coffee. But then you said you did not want to meet again! I can only assume that you are wary about relationships. My advice to you: you do not have forever, and at this stage of life you must surely realise that you need to take a few risks.*
> *Or maybe you are just a dreamer. Perhaps you are waiting for your perfect man. If so, "Donna Quixote", at this stage of life you need to drop some of your criteria for a partner. Otherwise you may find you'll be growing old alone. Time is running out, you know. If you are living in a fantasy world you need to be more realistic.*
> *In any case, you know I am well meaning. I hope to hear from you. And if not...well, just keep tilting at windmills!*
> *Gary*

Donna burst into laughter. What an arrogant man. He was obviously feeling cut that she didn't want to see him again. But if he needed to have the last word, so be it. She decided it was pathetic.

She went upstairs to put the last finishing touches to her makeup before heading off to Rick's for lunch with the girls

~~

Nina was already seated at their corner table when Donna and Trudy arrived at Rick's, and the others all arrived within a few minutes.

'Good to be back here among some sane people,' Donna declared.

'Why, who's been acting insane?' asked Paula.

Donna recounted to her friends her experience with Gary.

'And there was this other guy. You know, I saw his profile, and thought *wow!* Dream profile. Ticked all the boxes. Well educated, thoughtful, and saying all the right things. Beautifully written; he was articulate, seemed emotionally switched on. Sounded almost too good to be true. Read *so* well, I decided I'd contact him.' She paused. 'Well, it turned out he *was* too good to be true.'

'What happened?' asked Halle.

'It was weird. He responded fairly quickly. But the language was different to his profile. At first I thought maybe he must have written his email when he was very tired, 'cause I noticed it was written at three o'clock in the morning. Or even maybe he'd had too much to drink.' She shook her head bemusedly. 'But the other emails that followed didn't fit with his profile either. Not well written like you'd expect from a university-educated man. He wrote like English wasn't his first language. So I wrote back and asked him where he was born, and what his heritage was. He said that he was born in Sydney, but did his Masters in the States, at UCLA. No way that was true.'

'Sounds like he must have had someone else write his profile for him,' said Halle.

Donna nodded. 'Then I noticed *all* his emails were written at around three or four o'clock in the morning, and it dawned on me that he was not living in Glen Waverley like he'd said, but was overseas somewhere. And I noticed that his internet provider wasn't an Australian one. Of course I stopped writing immediately.'

'Sounds like a scam. I reckon the next step would have been some hard luck story, and a desperate request for a loan to get him out of a spot,' said Nina. 'I've heard that happens sometimes.'

'Yes, you're probably right. Anyway, then I noticed his profile disappeared for a while. A couple of weeks later I saw the exact same profile; well, the same words as before...but the photo was of a different man! And this time he said he lived in Prahran.' She paused, and shrugged. 'There sure are some strange ones out there. I know there are good guys too. But the trouble is when you meet on the internet you meet in a vacuum. You don't know anything about them other than what they choose to tell you.'

'Yeah, someone was telling me how some people create these avatars, they invent these whole imaginary personas,' Paula added. 'You need to be careful. It reminds me how lucky I was to meet Ted so quickly without having to deal with any of those shady characters.'

'I don't know how you can bear to do what you're doing,' said Halle. 'I'm so grateful I've met Sophia and I don't have to go through that. I admire you. You've got guts. I'd be too scared to put myself out there for experiences like you've had. First Harvey, and then profiles and emails like that...'

Donna laughed. 'You have to be on your toes. I'm learning a hell of a lot in a short time. But you know, it's a fascinating experience.' She was pensive. 'I didn't date much when I was young. Martin was it, basically.'

'Could you ever have imagined you'd be dating at this time in life?' asked Halle. 'I know I didn't.'

'No, never dreamed it. Sometimes I still can't believe I'm doing this at sixty. I feel like I'm on a roller coaster, and going on this big adventure ride. But I'm challenged by the ride. Even with the bumpy bits...even what happened with Harvey.' She smiled at the others. "And you know, I don't mind being *Donna Quixote*. Life is certainly not boring. It's a whole new chapter of my life. And maybe I *am* a dreamer. But you know what? That's okay.'

'Let's drink to this chapter,' said Nina, raising her glass. 'And to our *Donna Quixote*. And let's make sure we live page turners. We'll all get to the final page far too quickly, anyway. Let's make it a bloody good story along the way.'

Donna laughed, raising her glass. 'Thanks, guys.'

'And Halle, things are obviously going well with Sophia?' asked Paula.

'Couldn't be better. The only problem is Tilly. She's upset. She assumed once I ended it with Frida I'd get back on the straight and narrow.'

'What's her problem?' Nina looked annoyed. 'Why can't she be happy for you?'

Halle shrugged. 'It's not her perfect picture of how a mother's supposed to live her life.'

'For Christ's sake, Halle, I hope you're not going to let it get to you again like it did when she carried on about Frida,' snapped Nina. 'At least then I could understand she was upset about you splitting with her father, and was worried about him. But she's not a child, she knows enough about life, and she's got no right to be making these judgements. I wish she could be pleased to see you happy, like we are. And anyway, you've certainly got your life a lot more in order than she has.'

Halle shrugged. 'Yes, I know. I agree with you. And I can't let it get in the way. I'd much rather see her able to approve. But you know, I'm happier than I ever remember being. So I can't let her spoil it. I just wish she could be more pleased for me.'

'It's her problem if she can't, isn't it?' Nina didn't like Tilly, and she didn't hide it.

But then Nina hasn't had children, Donna thought, feeling protective of Halle. She just doesn't understand that strong filial connection, and so it was easy for her to dismiss Halle's desire for Tilly's acceptance. She suggested this to Nina, who merely shrugged and went silent.

At that moment their waitress appeared with a tray of port. 'Rick asked me to bring these over for you,' she offered.

Halle laughed. 'This is getting to be a very pleasant habit.'

The women started to sip their port, and the tension was soon allayed.

'What about you, Nina? How's it going for you?' Donna asked.

'Okay. I've been out with a couple more guys. Nothing significant to report.'

Donna sensed that Nina was holding something back. But glancing at her friend she decided not to ask. Donna knew she'd talk when she was ready. 'Well, time for me to rap it up,' she declared, looking at her watch. 'Shall we call for the bill?'

~~

Donna was silent for a few minutes as Trudy drove towards home. She could feel Trudy's eyes on her.

'Got something on your mind?'

'Just wondering about Nina. She didn't seem herself. Did you notice?' asked Donna.

'Yeah, you're right. Not her usual bubbly self. Hope everything is okay.'

'She's at a real fork in the road. She's got some big decisions to make.'

'Yes,' replied Trudy. 'I just hope she can end it with Tony and move on while she's still can. And of course she's aware of that, too.'

Donna's mobile rang, interrupting their conversation.

'Nina, you must have ESP. Trudy and I were just talking about you! Are you okay? Didn't want to push you during lunch but you seemed like you had something going on.'

She was silent, while Nina talked at the other end of the line. Then, 'Okay. Sounds like a good idea. I'll follow up on it this week.' There was a pause as Nina responded. Then Donna continued, 'Yeah, I get that. Much better coming from recommendation...No, I don't mind if you want to see Norm. I'll ask him when I see him. Some therapists don't like to see friends of their patients, but I'll check it out....No, I'm definitely okay with it, I'll feel better knowing you're in good hands....Okay, I'll work on it and we'll talk soon.   Sounds like a great move.   Are you alright?...You just didn't seem yourself...Okay...Bye.'

Trudy didn't say anything, waiting for Donna to speak.

'So you got that?'

'Yes. I'm pleased.' Trudy smiled. 'We must have been sending her vibes.'

'Yes, and I'm sure she's got more happening there than she's saying. But she'll tell us when she's ready.'

Chapter 16

Donna was at The Coffee Pot, a café she often enjoyed coming to on weekends. Feeling relaxed, she sat sipping her coffee, the Saturday Age spread out on the table before her. It was cold outside, but there was a log fire burning in the room.

She loved leisurely Saturdays like this, and working on the Samurai Sudoku was a regular weekend pastime. It was pretty frustrating, though, when she got it wrong. Sometimes she could work on the five interlocking puzzles for two hours, only to find she'd made a mistake somewhere. She was determined that wasn't going to happen this morning, though, as she slowly worked her way through it.

She felt someone looking at her, that sense you get before you even look up. She glanced around the room. That guy at the corner table. She'd noticed him earlier. She thought he might be a regular here too, like herself, because he looked familiar. He grinned, then looked away, embarrassed. He had a pleasant face. Probably late fifties or early sixties, she reckoned. Smiling to herself, she returned to her Sudoku. As the waitress wandered by she ordered another coffee. Trudy had said if she could make it she'd call in, too.

She heard her phone beep, indicating a new message. It was from Halle, who was organising a book club. The first meeting was scheduled to take place in three weeks time, and Halle wanted to let her know it was to be at her place. Donna sent a message back confirming that she'd be there.

Their first novel, *You Should Have Known,* was in her bag. She had started it earlier in the week, and was enjoying the psychological thriller. The theme intrigued her. The narrator, a psychotherapist, was releasing a book she'd written, based on her clinical experience, suggesting that with poor relationship choices the "signs" were always there right at the beginning, but people often failed to pay attention to what their intuition was telling them. She wondered whether *she* should have known in the early stages of her relationship with Harvey. Were there signs that she ignored? Had she been blind to any intuitive signals? Good to consider the possibility. She certainly didn't want to make the same sort of mistake again.

The man who'd smiled at her earlier was at the counter now, paying. As he made his way out of the café he nodded, almost shyly, at Donna. It was quite endearing, she thought, feeling flattered that he'd noticed her, and that she was not as invisible as she sometimes felt. She smiled back, then returned to her puzzle.

~~

After her second coffee she called Nina. She knew that her friend had been to see Norm during the week, and was keen to know how she'd gone.

'It went well. I felt pretty stirred up. But I suppose that's normal.'

'Yes, it is; we don't go into therapy to talk about the things that don't rouse us up,' Donna offered. 'Not always comfortable.'

'Yeah, I know. All that old shit from my childhood, though. I don't like revisiting that. But I did like Norm; and I think he'll be good for me. As long as you're sure you feel okay for me to see him. You still feel alright about it?'

'Yes, I thought about it some more after we spoke on the phone, and I talked it through in my session. It's all good. I'm sure he'll make a sane person out of you yet, you crazy gal,' she jested. 'And seriously, I'm sure you'll get a lot out of it.'

They chatted for a few more minutes, with Nina sharing some of what had taken place in her session. Then she suddenly said, 'Thanks. And by the way, you were right, I was holding back at our last lunch. I'll talk about it when I see you. I've got to rush now, there's the doorbell. I've got someone coming to look at some of my paintings. See you Saturday. Bye.'

'Bye,' Donna replied, but Nina had already hung up. It reminded her of how she sometimes brought up important material right at the end of a therapy session. Norm had pointed out to her that it was her way of letting him know about something when it was too late to go deeper. The late information dump. Unconscious, of course. Here's a hint of something that's important. Just a taste, sorry I don't have time to serve you up the whole meal.

She smiled to herself, feeling affection for Nina. It was strange in a way. Her friend was so outspoken, yet when it came to the more personal and emotional aspects of her life she tended to sometimes pull the shutters down. At least for a while, anyway. But then she did usually get around to talking about what was on her mind eventually. Perhaps it was Nina's need to feel in control. Donna thought she probably didn't like to talk about things while they were still unresolved. Nina hated feeling vulnerable, admitting it made her feel weak. It didn't fit with the way she liked to be seen.

Donna sighed, knowing it would be hard for Nina to be open to a full-on relationship without being more emotionally exposed. Donna had learned in her own life that if you're going to open your heart you're going to be vulnerable. And sometimes you got hurt.

Bruno Mars was lamenting his lost love in the background, When I Was Your Man. I should have been more thoughtful, the song's lyrics suggested. "I should have bought you flowers". "I should have held your hand". If only...

Ah yes, she remembered her own laments, and her own questioning after Martin left her. Could she have done things differently? For a long time she'd blamed herself for the demise of her marriage. She'd believe it had to be some sort of failing in her. It had to be her fault that Martin had gone off and looked for someone else. If only she'd been more...whatever...then it wouldn't have happened. Not so much now, though. She'd stopped accusing herself. Most of the time, anyway. Funny how changes creep up on you imperceptibly. In fact she was even getting to like who she was. Definitely a late bloomer, she decided.

She took a mouthful from the cheese and fruit plate she'd ordered, and took her book out. The place was filling up now with the lunch crowd.

'Sorry I couldn't make it sooner.' Her friend's voice interrupted her thoughts. She hadn't noticed Trudy making her way to the table.

'You're just in time to help me get through this plate before I make a complete pig of myself,' Donna answered.

'Well, let's forget the big breakfast I had with Alan, I'll just start all over again,' she laughed. 'Been here long?'

Donna looked at her watch. 'Yeah, a couple of hours. God, I don't know where that went. I hadn't realised. Lucky they haven't kicked me out.'

'You must have been behaving yourself moderately well.'

The two friends sat and enjoyed their comfortable banter. Donna looked fondly at Trudy. She was a gem. In fact, she reminded herself, she owed her life to Trudy. And life was looking pretty good these days.

~~

It was mid-afternoon and Donna was vacuuming. Well, life couldn't be all coffee and chat. It was probably just as well Trudy eventually broke up their get-together, or she might otherwise still have been out avoiding the housework.

She emptied the dishwasher, and started putting the dishes into their usual spots in the cupboard. As she reached, she noticed the salad bowl on the top shelf. It had been a wedding present. She tried to recall who had given it to them. Too many years ago now to remember. How long had it been since she'd used that bowl, with its multi-coloured mosaic pattern? It always reminded her of a kaleidoscope, and it had frequently brought positive comments when she and Martin used to entertain. It was beautiful, but she never used it these days. Not the sort of bowl you take out of the cupboard just for yourself.

Her thoughts meandered. All those dinner parties back then. Maybe it was time to do it again. She'd had the family for meals, and Trudy and Alan. But for the first time in years she found herself considering doing the whole dinner for ten deal (or nine, unless she could find a man she'd like to invite). It could be fun. She was already tossing around ideas in her mind about what she might cook.

It would be good to ask the Saturday lunch girls and their partners. Given the rustiness of her hostessing skills, they felt the safest and most comfortable candidates for her to break the drought. Besides, there was no-one she'd rather have there. She wondered who Nina might bring, or in fact whether she'd want to ask anyone at all. Hopefully not Tony, out on loan from his marriage!

She went to her diary to check a couple of potential dates for the dinner party. She'd check with the girls on Saturday.

Chapter 17

Donna looked at her watch. They were late arriving at Rick's. Paula had offered to pick her up, and had arrived a few minutes after the time they'd arranged. Donna knew she should curb her obsession with punctuality; after all, they were only a few minutes late. She made a silent note to herself to talk to Norm about it at her next session.

The others had all arrived.

'Hey there, you two. Just starting to get worried. We always know we can set our watches by you, Donna. As soon as it's five minutes after the arranged time we start to worry you must have been abducted,' laughed Halle.

'My fault,' Paula responded. 'Mia culpa.'

'It's probably good for me to try to let go of a tiny bit of my temporal OCD,' said Donna.

'We'll never cure you of that,' Halle laughed. 'One of the defining quirks we know and love about you.'

'Or in spite of,' Nina quipped. 'Anyway, I'm starving. Let's eat.'

The women perused their choices. Rick wandered over to say hello.

'So what are you going to have today?' he asked.

'Any recommendations?' asked Paula.

'There are a couple of specials. The osso bucco is good. Or if you feel like pasta the fetuccine with garlic prawns has been popular too.'

'Love the personal attention, Rick,' said Halle. 'You've obviously still got things in order out in the kitchen.'

'Yes, it's working well. And by the way, did I tell you I'm going to be closed for a few weeks next month? I'm starting renovations.

I'm very excited about it. I hope you'll love what I'm doing. And of course the painting should look fantastic.'

'Painting? What painting?' asked Paula.

Rick looked surprised. 'You don't know? Nina, you're too modest. You haven't told them?'

Donna glanced at Nina. Wasn't that a blush she was seeing on her usually inscrutable friend's face?

'I was going to surprise them,' she told Rick. 'But it was getting to be too hard to keep to myself, so I planned to tell them today.'

'I'll leave it to you, then,' Rick said. 'But it's looking sensational. You're very talented.' He gave Nina's shoulder a light squeeze before walking to another table.

Donna wondered if she was the only one to notice the slightly intimate gesture. Nobody commented.

'Okay, spill the beans. What's this about a painting?' asked Paula.

'Rick commissioned me to do it. We got talking one day when I stayed back after you guys had left, and he told me about the changes he wanted to make here. It just went from there, and he came around to see my work. He liked my paintings a lot, and asked me if I could make some suggestions for here. I've been working my butt off. It's almost finished. But I reckon I may have to be working through the night to get it done in time.'

'What are you painting?' asked Halle.

'It's a landscape. Italian, a Tuscan scene. Peaceful, pastel tones, a change of pace for me. Quite different from some of the colourful stuff I've been doing lately, but it feels good to have a change in direction. And it should fit in well with the theme Rick wants here.'

'I can't believe you've kept this under wraps. You're such a dark horse. How come you didn't mention it before?' questioned Halle.

Nina sat quietly, before finally speaking. 'Well...to tell you the truth, that's not all of it.' She stopped.

'So what's all of it?' asked Trudy.

'Well...Rick and I have...have sort of been seeing a bit of each other. When he came to my studio and we talked about the

97

painting, we just kept talking. We found we had a lot in common. And that we liked each other. I didn't want to mention it to you in the beginning. 'Cause you all know him, and I didn't know what was going to happen. You know my track record. You're all so used to my little interludes. This has felt different, but I haven't been able to trust it.' She was quiet for a while, then said to Donna, 'That's why I decided it was time for me to see someone, and why I asked you about Norm. You all know how I keep fucking everything up as soon as an available man takes any interest in me …and I didn't want to say anything in case I screwed up again.'

'Nina, that's terrific. All of it. The painting, and Rick. He's a great guy. I didn't know if he was in a relationship or not, but it sounds like he's actually available?' asked Halle.

'Yes, he separated from his wife about eighteen months ago.' She laughed. 'And one of the worst parts was, I kept saying to myself, "Shit, what happens if I muck this up? There go our beautiful lunches at Rick's". But we seem to be doing okay.' She paused. 'At least, I hope we are. I'm pretty anxious. He's had to deal with a couple of melt-downs already.'

'And Tony? Does he know?' asked Paula.

'Well…here's the news I know you guys have all been waiting for. I…I ended it with Tony a couple of weeks ago.'

'No kidding! That's fan-bloody-tastic,' Halle yelled out, then looked around the café to see if anyone had heard her outburst. 'How was it for you to end it?'

'Not as hard as I expected it to be. He was upset. But I knew I had to walk away. I did listen to what you were all telling me, and I knew you made sense, but I wasn't ready to face it before.'

'So are you okay about it now?' asked Donna.

'I actually feel relieved that I've done it.'

'Great!' said Paula. 'Good on you.'

'I just hope I don't go running scared again. That's why I thought I'd better do some real work on this…this stuff. All those workshops that I've been to forever obviously haven't been enough.

I know it's time to get into the nitty-gritty.' She grinned. 'So here I am. Feeling terrified at times. But Rick's been amazingly understanding.' She gave a nervous smile. 'I got scared shitless a couple of weeks ago when he asked me if I want to meet his son. Feels too serious and committed. I'm not sure I'm ready for that yet.'

'No need to rush things, is there?' asked Donna.

'No, that's what Rick said, too.'

'Let's have a glass of champagne to celebrate,' said Donna.

'What a good idea,' said Nina. 'Bring it on.'

'By the way,' said Donna. 'I'm having a dinner party. I want you all to come. Can we find a date that suits everyone? And Nina, now you can ask Rick to join us!'

~~

They were on their second bottle of bubbly. Donna was getting giggly. Nina was flushed and quieter than usual.

'What a bundle of surprises you've brought us today,' said Paula to Nina. 'First of all Rick, and the painting, and then getting rid of Tony.'

Nina grinned. 'Yeah, you're probably as surprised as me. Still pinching myself. But it's early days,' she added quickly, with an edge of urgency that seemed to say "don't see it as a done deal too quickly!"

'Yes, we get it,' said Halle. 'But I'm so pleased.'

Nina nodded, then added hurriedly, not wanting to dwell on her "bundle of surprises", 'I want to check out what's for desserts. Any of you interested?'

'Not for me,' said Paula, 'I've started on Lite N' Easy a couple of weeks ago, and don't want to go too far off track.' She smiled, adding, 'After you guys got stuck into me for considering the lap band option, I had a good talk to Ted. He agreed completely with you, and fortunately he loves me cuddly. But he said he'd help me lose some weight because I don't like it, and so we're both being careful. I've lost a couple of kilos already and I'm feeling better for it.

'Yes, I thought you looked like you'd lost some weight. It shows in your face. Still got those wonderful boobs that welcome us before the rest of your body, though,' laughed Nina. 'You're not allowed to lose any there. You're such a w-o-m-a-n', she spelled. 'I'd love some of that.' She was always lamenting her "little cherries", as she called them.

Paula laughed. 'Not much chance my balloons are going to deflate. But I feel good that I've started to do something about the rest of the bod.'

Trudy and Halle were engrossed in conversation down the end of the table. There was a silence, then Halle said, 'I was just talking about the blow up I had with Tilly this week. She started having a go at me again about Sophia, and I just lost it. I started yelling at her to butt out, and that I had no intention of ending my relationship or anything else I choose to do with my life. And things just continued from there. I told her I'm sick to death of supporting her lazy life style and that it was time for her to get off her bum and start doing something to take financial responsibility for herself. I said I won't do it any more. She got furious, and stormed out of the house. She made me so mad, telling me how to run my life and not doing enough with hers. I just boiled over.'

'Not before time,' said Nina. 'Good for you. She's taken advantage of your generosity for far too long. It's about time she had it spelled out. Have you spoken since?'

'No. I nearly picked up the phone last night, but stopped myself. I'm still feeling mad at her. She pushed all my buttons, trying to tell me I shouldn't choose to be with Sophia. But I'll contact her when I've cooled down a bit. I don't want World War Three with her. I love her to bits, but I'm very angry with her.'

'No, you've done her a favour,' said Trudy. 'She needs to know what it's like to take responsibility for her life. She can still pursue her writing if that's what she wants. But in her spare time. It'll be better for her to get more realistic about life.'

'Yes, I know.' Halle was crying now. 'I know you're right. I've always known you guys were right about me supporting her. And she just pushed me too far.' She paused, wiping away her tears. 'I've been so hurt that she can't be more pleased for me that I've found happiness. I've never felt like this before in my life. I just couldn't let her spoil it. And the rest just came pouring out. I've been more upset about being taken for granted than I realised.'

The women were quiet for a couple of minutes.

'Wow, it feels like a lot has happened this month,' said Paula, breaking the silence.

'Yeah,' agreed Nina. Then she said, 'Well, if we're going to order desserts I have to do it now. I've got a painting to finish.'

Chapter 18

Donna was getting dressed. Tonight she had a date with a man called Murray. She would have expected to feel more excited. They were meeting face to face for the first time. They'd been exchanging emails, and had talked a couple of times on the phone. He was a widower, with children around the same age as Becky and Luke.

She'd felt disappointed when he'd rung her. He had one of those high-pitched voices. She loved a deep voice on a man. But then she told herself not to be so judgemental. Murray seemed like a decent sort of person, from what she could gather.

She'd chosen her little black dress, one of the items from her new wardrobe of clothes. She was okay with how she looked. She was pleased she'd been on that shopping spree. It felt good to have new clothes to wear. She put on her new black shoes – "fuck me shoes", Nina had called them - did a quick check, picked up her keys and headed for the car. They'd agreed to meet halfway between his place in Fairfield and hers, at a Thai restaurant Murray had suggested.

True to form, she got there right on time, and found a parking spot right outside. A good omen? she wondered. She placed the high-pitched voice into the "disregard" basket. Not fair to hold that against him. She wondered what she sounded like on the phone. Maybe he was having to disregard the tone of her voice, too. Or some other annoying little quirk. Trivial, she told herself. She walked into the restaurant and looked around the dimly lit room. The man at a table midway into the restaurant smiled at her, indicating that he must be Murray. She smiled back, and walked over to him.

He reached towards her and took her hand. 'Donna? I'm so pleased to meet you. I've been looking forward to this all week.'

She felt guilty. He seemed nice, and she smiled back. 'And I'm pleased to meet you, too.' She wasn't lying. Looking at him, the timbre of his voice disappeared from her reckoning, and she saw a shy honesty. He had an open face, more warm than he'd looked in his photo.

He had a bottle of wine on the table. He'd checked with her beforehand what she liked to drink. 'Ready for a glass?' he asked. 'I've already started, as you can see. I got here early. And I have to admit I felt a little nervous. I'm not used to doing this. I haven't dated for forty years. I'm feeling like a kid all over again.' He laughed, and she warmed to him some more.

Over dinner Donna found he was intelligent, with a broad general knowledge, and once Murray relaxed a little she enjoyed their conversation.

'I can't believe I'm doing this internet thing,' he laughed. My daughter persuaded me to give it a try. I felt a bit weird about it, but thought why not give it a go? And here we are. I must say I'm glad she suggested it now, though. We wouldn't have met otherwise.'

'Same story for me. My daughter nudged me to do it, too. She helped me put together my profile. I had no idea that people our age would be doing this.'

'Yes…sometimes I can't believe that I *am* this age.'

'I know what you mean. I'm not sure where the years have gone.'

Murray grinned. 'I grow old, I grow old, I shall wear my trousers rolled.'

Donna laughed, then said, 'Prufrock. That happens to be one of my favourite poems.'

'Yes, mine too. I'm not ready to roll up my trousers yet, though. Lots of living still to do.' He was pensive. 'It was a real wake-up call when my wife died. There were so many things on our "to do" list that we didn't have a chance to do. We take our life and our health so much for granted. Since she died I'm much more

tuned into living each day. But sometimes it gives me a shock to realise how fast the months are flying by, and I just want to get the most out of every bit of life while I can.' He was pensive.

'"And at my heels I always hear time's winged chariot drawing near",' said Donna.

'Hey, we're really on a roll! Marvell. I *love* that poem, too.' He looked surprised, obviously pleased she knew it. 'You like poetry?'

'Yes, a lot.'

The conversation flowed, as they talked animatedly about Shakespeare, and a diverse range of novels, poetry and plays.

'You know a lot about literature,' she commented.

He laughed. 'I hope so. I lecture in English at university.'

'You do?' Donna was fascinated, and thrilled that she had a welcome space to discuss one of her favourite topics. In spite of her early misgivings the evening was proving to be most enjoyable.

But she found a battle going on within. She kept telling herself that he was a good man. Intelligent. And interesting. Someone who'd probably treat her very well. But there was absolutely no spark. She wondered if that could build. After all, this was the first time they'd met.

When they finished dinner Murray looked at his watch. 'My God, that time just flew. Time's winged chariot again. It's eleven o'clock. I feel like we've only been here for a couple of hours but in fact it's nearly double that.' He was quiet for a moment. She didn't answer him, so he went on, 'Donna, I enjoyed this. I'd like to see you again. Could we have dinner again soon?'

He was good company, so after hesitating briefly while the internal battle continued, Donna agreed to his suggestion, and they arranged a night that suited them both the following week.

'I'll call you in another day or two. Thanks for a lovely night.'

'Thank you for dinner. And yes, it was lovely. We'll talk soon, then.'

He walked her back to her car, and gave her a gentle kiss on the cheek. Donna was grateful that he hadn't tried anything more adventurous.

~~

The phone rang twice before she answered. Trudy was seated opposite her, sipping coffee. It was Murray, wanting to confirm their dinner date. Donna hesitated, wondering if she should tell him about her reservations, but decided to meet with him again before deciding what to do. They arranged that this time he'd pick her up from home, and she hung up with Murray telling her how much he was looking forward to seeing her again.

Trudy didn't say anything, but raised her eyebrows in silent enquiry.

'Well, as you probably heard, that was Murray.'

'Yes. But you weren't exactly jumping out of your chair with excitement. I've seen more enthusiasm in a dead fish.'

'Oh God, was I awful to him? He's a good guy, I don't want to be mean to him.'

'No, you weren't mean,' answered Trudy. 'I just know you so well, and I know when you're keen and when you're not.'

'Trouble is, he's so damn nice. I wish I felt more chemistry. But it just wasn't there. And I don't want to lead him down a dead end street. I thought maybe the fireworks might happen later rather than sooner. Or maybe I'm expecting too much at this stage of my life. Maybe I've lost it. Maybe Harvey was a one off thing.'

Trudy laughed. 'Come on, that's bullshit; you know there's still a woman alive and well and living in that body of yours. You felt it with Harvey and you'll feel it again. It'll be there with the right person. But you know what, if it isn't there with Murray it just isn't there. You can't manufacture it. It's a pity, because he does sound like a decent guy. Decency's a necessary but not sufficient ingredient, though.'

'Yes, you're right,' said Donna. 'But I don't want to hurt him,.'

'Just tell him the truth. And who knows, he could be a friend even if there's no romance there.'

'That's true. That feels better.'

~~

Donna had finished her main course. She and Murray had again had a pleasant evening, and had shared a lot about themselves. She enjoyed their conversation.

She took a deep breath. 'Murray, I need to be honest with you. I enjoy your company. A lot. But I don't see us as a couple…a romantic couple. I do like you so much, and I don't want to mislead you.'

Murray didn't answer immediately. Then he swallowed, and said, 'I enjoy your company, too. We get on well. And I can't pretend that I'm not disappointed, because I was hoping that something could develop here. But thank you for your honesty.' He hesitated, then continued, 'And I don't know how you feel about this, but it seems like a pity to just not see each other any more. So…how would you feel about us still catching up sometimes? I like talking to you. Maybe we could go to a film or a play from time to time, or catch up for a meal.'

Donna smiled, feeling a warmth towards him. 'That would be great. I feel the same way. And thanks for being so understanding.'

He looked at her, not answering immediately, then lifted his glass. 'So here's to friendship.'

'To friendship.'

It was a pity, because her head told her that he would have been kind to her…and honest. But her heart wouldn't follow. A good man. "Necessary but not sufficient". She'd have to remember that.

Chapter 19

Donna smiled as she closed her laptop. Unbelievable. She was being inundated with emails from prospective suitors. There'd been four more "hugs" and a couple of emails waiting for her when she checked her emails. Three of them she'd declined immediately. One of them from a forty-two year old. *Another* young one. She didn't understand. What were they on about, these young men responding to the profile of a woman nearly twenty years older than them? Mother complex? Or looking for an older woman with money? She'd heard that happened sometimes.

The other two just had no appeal at all. No shared interests, and seemingly quite different to her. Delete, delete, delete.

She'd been corresponding with three men. One of them had asked her if she'd like to have lunch with him the following week. They'd spoken on the phone a couple of times. He was a company director who'd done a lot of travel and sounded interesting. She wrote a short email, saying she'd like to meet him, and asked him if he could suggest a venue.

The second man was a retired airline pilot. She didn't know much about him yet. She re-read his profile; he seemed okay from what she could judge. She wrote a quick email, suggesting they have a phone conversation the following night, then pressed the "send" button.

The third man she'd felt a little intrigued with. She'd sent a "hug" to him about three weeks ago, but hadn't had an email response until today. She re-read his message.

Hi CheekyChic,
Thanks for contacting me. It was good to hear from you. I'm sorry it has taken me time to get back to you. I felt interested to read your profile. But I've hesitated to respond to your message because I very recently formed a relationship with a woman who is living overseas. But it seems like you and I might have a lot in common, and if you feel comfortable about it I would love to meet you for a coffee, and have a chat. Who knows, we might find that we can have a friendship. Let me know what you think. I hope to hear from you soon.
Meanwhile,
Regards,
Art.

She phoned Trudy. 'He sounds so interesting. He's a writer and actor.'

'Hm. I'm not sure. He's already in a relationship. What's the point? Are you sure you're okay with friendship?'

'Well, that's what I've done with Murray. It's nice to have someone to go to a movie or dinner with sometimes. I'd like to meet this guy.'

'I don't know. I'm not comfortable about you getting caught up with him. He isn't available for a relationship.'

'I'm not exactly getting caught up with him. We're only talking about coffee.' She was aware she'd snapped at Trudy. Unusual for her.

'It's your call. I just don't want to see you getting hurt again.'

Donna didn't answer for a moment. 'Yeah, I get what you're saying. But it's just a coffee. I'm sure I'll be able to tell pretty quickly if he seems genuine.'

'I just can't see why you'd bother. And besides, why the hell is his profile still up there if he has someone in his life?'

'I'm not sure. Anyway, I'll think about what you've said.'

Later over dinner Donna reflected on her conversation with Trudy. Did she want another male friend? Finally, she decided why not? And Art wasn't lying about where he was at, like Harvey. He was up front.

She emailed him, thanking him for his honesty, and saying she liked the idea of coffee and friendship. He wrote back almost immediately, and they arranged to meet at a cafe not far from her house.

~~

She sat sipping her second cup of coffee. She looked across at Art. He was American, originally from New York, with the gift of the gab, like a lot of New Yorkers. He wasn't a good-looking man. And quite short, shorter than her. But there was something about him. She was intrigued. She found herself laughing a lot.

They talked about their marriages. They'd both been divorced for about the same number of years. After they'd chatted for over an hour she said to him, 'We're still such strangers. We've been talking about our lives but you don't even know my surname.' She told him, and he looked intently at her.

'What's the matter?' she asked.

'That's a pretty unusual surname. You said your husband's name was Martin. I...I don't suppose he's got a relative called Dan?'

'Yes...his brother is Dan.'

'Married to Barbie? They live in Sydney?'

Donna stared at him incredulously. 'Yes. You know them?'

'Unbelievable. Talk about six degrees of separation!'

Art then told her about a holiday he and his ex-wife had been on with Dan and Barbie several years ago. 'We knew them well. We used to mix in the same circle of friends. Now that we're talking about it, I've got a vague memory that he used to talk about Martin. But after my divorce we lost contact, and I came down to Melbourne to live.'

They discovered that they knew other people in common. Donna found herself pleasantly thrown. But she noted that this was mixed with a mild caution. She knew Trudy meant well, but she wished she hadn't put doubts in her mind. He was good company. Still, she knew her friend had a point.

'How come you still have your profile up on the internet if you've met someone?' she asked him.

'Yes, I must remove that. I just hadn't gotten around to it yet. But you're the only one I've agreed to meet with since I met Felicity. Just something about your profile made me feel like we'd get on well.'

He seemed sincere. She shrugged off her concern and let herself enjoy his company, deciding that she was probably being silly. Perhaps it was the synchronicity that was unsettling: it was amazing that he'd known her ex in-laws, and other people from her past. 'I can't believe those coincidences, the people we both know. Incredible.'

'Yeah.' He was silent, then looked at her. 'You know, I feel so comfortable with you. In other circumstances I have a feeling we might have hit it off even more. Time's a funny thing. If I'd met you just a couple of months ago before I met up with Felicity...who knows what might have happened.' He tilted his coffee cup at her. 'Anyway, here's to friendship.'

'To friendship.'

They were both silent for a while. Then Donna asked him, 'Have you always been an actor and writer?'

'No, I worked in the corporate world until a couple of years ago. Then I had a serious falling out with the CEO and ended up losing my job.' He hesitated. 'I've got a habit of shooting from the hip that gets me into trouble sometimes. When that happened I looked at it as an opportunity to re-consider what to do with my life. It's been a disastrous couple of years, but I'm enjoying this new experience, too. Maybe I'll get back to that other world again, because I'm not exactly raking in the dollars at the moment. Who knows, though, I've got a few possibilities in the wings. Maybe I'll make it with this new TV show I'm working on. I had some interest expressed at Channel Nine.' He was silent for a moment. 'But it's a tough industry, and I must admit I don't fancy the idea of being a poor writer.'

Donna nodded. 'How did you meet Felicity?'

'I met her through friends. Actually, we discovered that we'd met a few years earlier through work. She was visiting from New York, and our paths crossed briefly, but we were both married at the time. He laughed. 'Strange meeting again like that. Another coincidence. Seems to be the theme of the day.' He paused. 'She comes from a fabulously wealthy family, well established in the international corporate world, and when we met a few weeks ago she was on a business trip. We only had a couple of weeks before she had to fly back home. We've talked every day since. Thank goodness for Skype!' He paused. 'I'm going back to New York in December; my younger daughter is getting married there, so I'll be able to spend some time with Felicity. It will be an opportunity to see if we do like each other as much as we thought.'

'Yes, it will be a good chance to get to know each other better.' Donna smiled. 'It certainly sounds like it's been a whirlwind romance.'

Art smiled at her. 'Yeah.' He glanced at his watch. 'I'm going to have to go.' He hesitated, then asked her, 'What are you doing tomorrow? The Fringe Festival is on. I don't suppose you'd be interested in coming with me?'

Donna hesitated, then shrugged. 'Sounds good. And I'm free. What time did you have in mind, and where will we meet?'

'How about I pick you up about one o'clock, if you're okay about telling me where you live. It's going to be hard to park, and it seems silly to take two cars. We can have a coffee or a bite to eat afterwards.'

'Okay.' She gave him her address and he gave her a polite kiss on the cheek before walking away. She sat for a while after he left, finishing her coffee and contemplating what had just happened.

Chapter 20

Donna was at Trudy and Alan's. They'd invited her over for an impromptu meal. They'd finished eating, and now Donna loaded dishes into the dishwasher while Trudy made coffee.

'Not bad for a thrown together meal,' Donna said.

Trudy laughed. 'Yes, I meant it when I said it. But I just got carried away.'

'I suppose I used to throw together a meal like that once, but I'm so out of touch now. I'm looking forward to my dinner party, but I must admit I'm nervous about it, too. I'm impressed with how easy you make it look. Your meals are always delicious.'

'It gives me something to do. To tell you the truth, I'm bored. Since I sold the Home and Garden shops I often don't know what to do with myself. Twenty years of that, I got used to having my days full. Buying, and managing and running between the shops to make sure everything was going smoothly. My days are feeling a bit empty now. So it's good for me to get busy with something.'

'Ever consider going back to work?'

'No, can't say it appeals to me. I don't want to get too involved in the business world again.'

'Well just keep cooking for me, Trude. I love your thrown together meals.'

'We love having you here. I wish you'd pop in more often.' She laughed. 'Alan is seeing more of you than I do now. He's thrilled to have you working there, by the way. He said you've fitted into the role perfectly.'

Donna smiled warmly at her friend. 'That's so good to hear. It was a life saver; I was going crazy at home, so I know what you're talking about.'

Trudy nodded. 'So how did your coffee date go today?'

'Very well. He's so interesting, and we had a terrific talk.' She told Trudy about the synchronistic links in their lives. 'And he talked about Felicity – that's the woman overseas –openly. Quite upfront about it.' She paused. 'We're…we're catching up again tomorrow to go to the Fringe Festival.' She noted the concern on Trudy's face. 'It's okay, you don't need to get that look again. We enjoy each other's company and we both felt a strong connection. I've got a feeling things could have been different if he hadn't met her; but he did, and is committed to pursuing that. We're both clear about that.'

Trudy nodded, but said nothing.

'Hm, that's a pregnant pause. It's okay, Trude. Come on, let's have this coffee.'

~~

Art arrived right on time. Big tick there, thought Donna. Maybe he was a punctuality freak like her.

It had been cold early in the morning, but by the time they walked to his car the sun had peeped through and hinted at a warmer day to follow.

'I looked forward to seeing you again after yesterday,' said Art. 'In fact I confess I even felt a bit of schoolboy excitement.'

Donna didn't answer.

'Did I make you uncomfortable when I said that?'

'Just confused.' She laughed. 'I suppose it's okay to get excited to catch up with a new friend.'

'Come on, let's go. We've got a lovely afternoon ahead of us.' He looked at her intently. 'I'm sorry, I didn't mean to confuse you.'

Donna took a deep breath. 'Okay. Let's go see what the Fringe Festival has to offer us.'

~~

'Would you like a coffee? Or would you like something stronger?' asked Art.

They were sitting by the window in a crowded café in Brunswick St. They'd walked, listened to music – Donna had to admit she'd found some of it too loud - taken in the sights for the last couple of hours and had already stopped once for coffee.

'A Shiraz would be wonderful now.'

Art smiled. Donna looked at him. What was there about this man that she found appealing? He had a crooked smile. He was balding, and when a breeze blew it stood on end. She found it comical, and grinned.

'What's funny?'

'The wind's just blown your hair on end, and it just made me smile. It reminded me of a cockatoo or a clown. Just tickled my fancy.'

He took it in good humour, and laughed with her. 'Just call me Bozo.'

A band Donna hadn't heard of before was playing in Brunswick Street, and she was enjoying herself. They were playing some mellow jazz. This was more to her liking. She looked around at some of the youths thronging the street. Would she like to be young again? Probably not, she decided. She'd been such an unsophisticated adolescent. Was it George Bernard Shaw who'd said "youth is wasted on the young"? There was a lot of truth in that, she decided.

Their wine arrived, and she sat back, sipping and enjoying the late afternoon buzz of the festival.

'I've had such a great day.'

'It's not over yet,' he said. 'I thought we might go to one of my favourite bistros for dinner, if that's still okay with you?'

Donna smiled and nodded her approval.

'Let me know when you get hungry.'

She loved listening to his stories, and there were many of them. From time to time they sat quietly, but before long Art would have another anecdote to tell her. She learned of his life as a young boy growing up in New York. Nearly getting expelled for the pranks he liked to play.

'A bunch of us decided to put sugar in our Science teacher's petrol tank. Nice guy, but ultra-conservative and he had no idea how to handle us. We gave him hell. He used to drive this tiny little Fiat K, his pride and joy. One day when we knew there was a teachers' meeting it was parked in the school car-park. A bunch of us lifted it and carried it from the car-park up the stairs and left it on the top landing. There was one hell of an uproar. And, being the ringleader, I was called into the chief's office the following day and that was nearly the end of my time at that school.'

He told her about his early enjoyment of the stage in school plays. 'That was where my love of acting started. Sometime I wish I'd pursued the dream more. I had fantasies back then of making it to the big screen. The arrogance of youth. I did make some efforts, but I soon realised I wasn't destined to be the next Paul Newman. So it's often amateur theatre now. Good for the soul, but not the pocket.'

Donna heard about his decision to come to Australia after he met Helen, who he married. The birth of his two daughters. And his divorce eight years ago. He enjoyed talking, and Donna enjoyed his stories.

He looked at her and suddenly said, 'It doesn't feel like we only met yesterday.'

'Strange, isn't it? I feel the same.'

Both were silent for a minute.

'Want another wine?'

'Let's go and get something to eat,' she replied.

Dinner was thoroughly enjoyable. They'd chatted almost non-stop, and Cicciolina, Art's favourite place in Acland St. was destined to be a popular place for Donna, too, she decided. 'That's one of the best meals I've had in a long time,' she told him. 'Nearly as good as the company.'

'Good. We'll have to do it again some time.' He looked straight into her eyes. It was a long intense look that left Donna feeling just a little unsettled.

'Are you alright?' he asked.

'Yes. I'm alright.'

'Ready to go?'

'Yes. Ready to go.'

~~

They drove to Donna's house.

'Do you want to come in for a coffee? Or are you all coffee'd out?' she asked. 'We can have a Bailey's if you'd prefer. What do you like to drink after dinner?'

'Bailey's sounds good.'

Donna realised as she was opening her front door that she was feeling slightly shaky. She felt an unnerving connection with this man. She took a deep breath. Art had his hand on her shoulder as she turned the key and stepped inside, with him following close behind.

'Do you want to sit in the lounge while I get the glasses?' she suggested, pointing him in the right direction.

She got ice out of the fridge to add to their drinks, took two glasses from the sideboard, and placed them on a tray with the bottle of Bailey's. He stared at her as she walked in and placed the tray on the coffee table, then quietly took her hand.

Donna knew there was an undeniable attraction between them. She said nothing, and after a few seconds removed her hand from his. 'Do you like ice in your Bailey's?'

He nodded, and she poured their drinks.

As they sat sipping, she felt as if his eyes could see right through her. 'So what are we going to do about this?'

She shrugged. 'Nothing. You've got Felicity, and you're not available for anything other than being my friend.'

'You're right. But we both know there's a strong connection here, don't we?'

She nodded. Neither of them spoke for a while, but the sexual tension was obvious.

'We can't be lovers,' she said quietly.

'You're right. We can't be lovers.' He sipped his wine. 'I can't give you what you deserve. And I don't want to do the wrong thing by you – ever. I like you. We obviously feel very attracted to each other, but there seems to be much more than that between us. I feel like I've known you before.' He gave her that intense look again. 'Donna, I don't want to ever hurt you.'

She looked at him and said, 'Please promise me something. Don't ever lie to me. That's really important.'

'I promise you, I'll never lie to you.'

She believed him. They sat close to each other, and the next hour seemed to fly quickly as they shared bits and pieces of their history. Suddenly he leaned across and kissed her. It was just a short kiss, but it left her shaky.

'I've been wanting to do that since that first cup of coffee,' he said. 'I know this sounds weird. We've only just met. But I'm falling for you.' He paused. 'Timing is a crazy thing. I know it would have been different if I'd met you earlier.'

She looked into his eyes, and saw the conflict sketched across his face. 'We need to put the brakes on; we both know we can't take this any further.'

'You're right. Just as well one of us is sensible.'

She looked at the clock. 'We'd better call it a night. It's nearly one o'clock. I have an appointment in the morning.'

'Okay. I'm ready to be thrown out. But…can I see you tomorrow night?'

Donna only hesitated for a moment. 'Yes, sure. What time? And where?'

'How about you come to my place and let me cook you a casual meal? And maybe we can watch a DVD.' And I promise to behave myself.' He grinned at her. 'At least, I'll try to, anyway.'

He gave her his address and left after kissing her again one more time.

As she arrived back home, Donna was tingling, her body alive with a passion that she hadn't expected to feel again. Or certainly not so soon. *Or* with someone who was already attached to another woman. She looked at herself in the mirror, barely knowing the woman who stared back at her.

Chapter 21

She arrived at Art's place at seven thirty. He opened the door, and politely welcomed her; then a smile spread across his face as he pulled her towards him and gave her a hug, which he broke very quickly.

'Come on in. I hope you're not expecting anything too grand. I promise you, I'm no gourmet cook.'

He led her into the lounge room. Donna looked around. Good taste. His furniture was simple but elegant, and he had a couple of fine paintings on the wall.

'All bought before my financial fall from grace,' he said to her, as if reading her mind. He pointed to the CD player, a pile of CD's beside it. 'Can you pick something you'd like to listen to and put it on while I bring in some pate and biscuits?' he asked.

Donna nodded. She headed to the CD player while he went in to attend to food. She selected an Eva Cassidy disc, and put Song Bird on the player.

'Do you want red or white wine?' he called from the next room.

'Red please.'

He sat opposite her when he came back with pate and dips.

Through dinner they kept away from any personal discussion. Art had prepared a meal of pepper steak and vegetables. The steak was cooked medium rare, just as she liked it. Donna complimented him.

They talked animatedly through dinner. But over coffee Donna felt herself getting flushed and anxious. She finished her drink. 'Art, that was wonderful. But I'm going to go now. I don't want to make this any more complicated.'

'Okay. I don't want you to go, but I understand. I'd love to see you tomorrow night though.'

'You don't reckon we should push the pause button?'

'Probably.' He stared at her, with a look she could only interpret as love, then drew her to him. 'Donna, I'm feeling totally thrown by you. I'm falling for you. I don't know what we're going to do. I feel guilty, because I'm an honest man.'

They locked eyes, and again she read his conflict. She knew she was throwing caution aside. Against all wisdom, she leaned forward and kissed him.

'This is crazy,' she told him.

'Yes, it's crazy. But we can spend the whole of our lives being sensible and we might just miss out on something special. There's something here, and I'm sure it's not just about sex.'

'No, it would be so much easier if it was.'

Neither of them spoke for a while. Art looked confused and distressed. A couple of times he repeated 'What are we going to do?'

Donna could hardly bear to see his pain. She didn't have an answer to his dilemma. She put her hand to his cheek and kissed his troubled eyes, then his cheeks and lips.

He took her hand, and without either of them speaking she followed him into the bedroom. He slowly undressed her, kissing her all the while. She was beyond trying to resist what they both felt, and she let herself submit to what felt like an almost intolerable passion between them.

In the early hours of the morning they realised they were both awake. They made love again. They slept a while. She heard him wake and get out of bed, then he returned a little while later. She curled up next to him and they both slept restlessly until the morning light stirred them.

When she got up her eyes spoke of too little sleep. Art kissed her, and said, 'I've got a couple of things on in the next couple of days. But I'll phone you.'

~~

They didn't see each other the following day. Art told her he had an appointment with someone about the show he was trying to sell to one of the TV channels, and he had another arrangement in the evening.

In her therapy session that day she could speak of nothing else.

'I'm feeling afraid,' she told Norm.

'What are you afraid of?'

'Well, I don't *really* know this man. He could be conning me, like Harvey did. How do I know? I've only known him a few days, after all. I'm afraid I could end up with egg on my face.' She hesitated. 'But I don't think so. There's been no subterfuge. He's been upfront about his situation. But I have moments when I'm scared I could end up totally devastated.'

'So given those fears, are you still prepared to keep going with this?' Norm asked.

Donna did not hesitate, even for a moment, before answering, 'Yes. I feel like I'm on a fast train, and there's no way I could, or would want to, get off.'

'So you're going along for the ride, no matter what.'

Donna nodded, looking at Norm's face, unable to read what he was thinking. He often did that, waiting to hear her thoughts rather than offering his own. And she knew whatever he thought now, she was not getting off the train. It was too tantalising a ride.

~~

It was Friday morning, and Donna was getting ready for work. She gazed outside. It looked cold, and the weather forecast had said it was going to get colder. She took her black jacket out of the cupboard, and put it on.

The phone rang. It was Art. 'We need to talk,' he said.

"*We need to talk.*" What did that mean? 'Well I'm off to work now. What about tonight?'

'Okay. Do you want to come over here?'

They arranged to meet at seven.

Donna rushed out to her car. She'd be a few minutes late getting to the clinic now. Her hand was shaking a little as she turned the key in the ignition and her stomach felt like a tumble drier. She maneuvered her way through the traffic, then realised with a shock as she pulled up into the clinic car-park that she barely remembered any of the drive there. She'd been completely absorbed in her thoughts. Maybe he'd told Felicity about them. Perhaps he'd ended the relationship and wanted to share what had happened with her.

She tried not to keep anticipating what he had to say. Norm would be telling her again that this was Act One, Scene One, and that she mustn't be jumping to Act Three. But she wished Art had told her on the phone. Now she was going to have to sit with this anxious feeling all day.

Fortunately the busy-ness of the clinic took over, and she managed to distract herself from her mind for at least part of the day.

~~

Seven o'clock, on the dot as always, Donna pushed the doorbell. She wished she could stop shaking.

'Hello.'

Still that worried look on his face as he invited her inside. That same tormented expression she'd seen previously. She wanted to hold him and comfort him.

'What do you want to drink?' he asked.

'Shiraz?'

Art didn't answer, but went to the other room, returning a short while later with a drink for each of them. He sat opposite her, his drink on the coffee table untouched for a couple of minutes, just staring at her.

'Donna, I've had to make a decision.'

Act One, Scene Two. A play filled with suspense.

'You know, when I met Felicity a little while ago, I felt something I hadn't felt for a long time. Perhaps only once before when I met Helen. And now I'm beginning to feel that same feeling with you, too. I'm falling in love with you, and I'm in danger of finding myself in the unenviable position of being in love with two women. And I've been worrying how if I allow that to happen…if that happens we're all going to lose out.'

He paused, staring at her. What was that look? Donna didn't know how to interpret it.

'I had a call from Felicity last night. She wants to come here to see me soon. In fact she's talking about permanently relocating so that we can be together. I didn't sleep last night, I realised I can't let this thing with you progress any more. I felt committed to Felicity, and meeting you has complicated my life. I knew I had to make a choice.'

Donna swallowed hard, staring at him. The interpretation was becoming clearer, and she didn't like it. She'd known this was a possibility, but she knew now that she'd bargained on having more time with Art before his visit to New York in December, and had thought that their developing relationship would surely consolidate in that time.

Donna felt tears brimming, and pushed them back. 'Well, I don't want to give up so easily,' she heard herself say. She barely recognised her voice. 'I think we've got something.'

Art stared at her. 'Don't make this any harder, Donna, please. I've made my decision. I thought about it long and hard, believe me, and it wasn't easy. I weighed up all the pros and cons. They had nothing to do with you or how much I feel for you. But I have to honour my commitment to Felicity. I'm sorry, I didn't want to hurt you.'

She felt the tears she'd tried to push back now stubbornly flowed. Art came and sat next to her, putting his arms around her.

'I'm sorry. I'm so sorry, I didn't want this to happen,' he repeated over and over.

Then he kissed her and said softly, 'I want to make love to you so much.' He stared at her. 'But this has to be the last time. It's better for both of us.'

Donna hesitated for only a moment, then felt herself submitting to his words. Surely he'd realise what they had together.

They made love on the couch. She stayed the night, but barely slept. In the morning they drank coffee together, and he told her some of his funny stories. She laughed, but felt battered inside. At one stage he caught the tears in her eyes, but no comment was made by either of them. He told her the first thing he'd be doing was to remove his profile from all the dating agencies he'd previously been on.

'I don't want to have anyone else get hurt like you have. And there's no reason for me to be up there online. I just didn't get around to removing them before.'

Donna nodded. She felt in a daze. She finished the last of her coffee. 'I have to get into the office.' She stared at him. 'So what happens now?'

'I'd love us to stay in touch, and I still want us to be friends if you would agree to that.'

'I don't know how that will be, and whether it can work, but I'd like to try,' Donna said.

She made her way to her car, Art just behind her. He kissed her on the cheek. 'How about I phone you soon and we'll have coffee or dinner?'

'Okay. Give me a call.'

She drove away, feeling numb, almost as if she were surrounded by cotton wool. Nothing felt real.

Chapter 22

'Thank God for the effects of alcohol. I don't know how I'd have managed sometimes,' said Donna, now on her second glass of wine. She'd just spilled out details of what had happened to Trudy, who'd sat quietly, listening to her outpourings.

'Want something to soak up the wine?'

Donna shook her head. 'No. I prefer the effects of the alcohol.'

'So where are you now? You seem pretty distraught.'

'Of course. What the hell would you expect?'

'Well if it were me I'd be damn furious. I feel full of rage just listening to you. Never mind he "didn't have time to remove his profile". Any decent guy just wouldn't have let you fall into that if he was so committed to someone else. And what the fuck were the "pros and cons" he was talking about, anyway? Are you sure it wasn't about her belonging to a "fabulously wealthy family"? You said he was pretty broke. You know that's what some people look for, don't you? There's something pretty suspicious about the whole deal. And have you looked to see if he has removed his profile?'

'No, I haven't been near the damn thing. Can't bear to look at it. But I will check it out. I couldn't believe it was deliberate, and I'm sure he would have taken it off by now. Not everyone is a Harvey, you know!' Donna responded, the edge of frustration with her friend in her voice.

'I know it's hard for you to hear what I'm saying. You know I'm on your side; I just hate the idea of you letting any bastard hurt you. It just doesn't sound kosher to me. Has he called you like he said he would?'

'No. I have been upset he hasn't called just to see if I'm okay. He knew how distressed I was. But perhaps he just wants to let me have some space for a while.'

Trudy sighed.

'What's the matter?' asked Donna.

'Christ, Donna, get real! I know you don't like it when I talk like this, but sometimes I want to shake you. Why are so willing to give him the benefit of the doubt?' You're in fantasy land sometimes. I don't want to be preaching "I told you so", but you knew the guy was not available. I hate seeing what you're doing to yourself. You need someone who can give you what you need, instead of falling for these shits.'

Donna stared at her friend, tears threatening to spill over.

'You know what I'm talking about. You need to be more cautious, and stop choosing no-hopers. You're much too good for these sorts of shenanigans. At least you know there *are* good men like Murray out there. I know the zing's not there with him, but you can tell he *is* genuine. And somewhere there'll be someone like that who you *do* feel attracted to.'

'God, I hope so.' Donna was silent for a moment, reflecting on what Trudy had been saying. 'I'm starting to doubt myself and my ability to judge. Actually, that's one of the things I've been struggling with this week. That's two guys – apart from Martin – who've let me down. Maybe I'm just not good at picking up the signs.'

'Well, maybe there's something to that. Sometimes we see what we want to see and miss out on what's actually there.'

'Yeah.' It was uncomfortable to confront this in herself, but then again she didn't want this to happen to her time after time. And she knew Trudy was right. The voice of reason. Even though she hated hearing her sometimes she knew she could always rely on Trudy to get her back on track.

~~

Donna opened her laptop, and hesitatingly entered the One Plus One site. Art would surely have done what he promised her he would do. There couldn't be another bastard like Harvey. She entered his pseudonym, tentatively. But he wasn't there. She sighed, relieved. She knew he wasn't like that.

She was about to shut the computer, but decided to try Mate-matches, another site he'd mentioned he'd been on. She entered the pseudonym he'd used on One Plus One, and was pleased to find it wasn't there.

She scrolled down the profiles, noticing a couple of familiar faces. She decided to look through to see if there were any others she knew, or any that seemed interesting. A band-aid for the wounded soul. A reminder there is life after Art. And Harvey. And Martin.

She read a couple who seemed interesting. Maybe she should try this site as well? Although on the other hand she wasn't sure she wanted to do any more of this. Too difficult. Nevertheless she kept scrolling.

She was lingering over one of them. Strange. Her skin prickled as she read. She couldn't believe what she was seeing. All too familiar! Actor. Writer. The pseudonym was different. It was a set of initials. ALB. Art Lionel Brunner! Then the header: *Available but choosy*.

She felt a stab of pain, then realised he must have just not gotten around to removing his profile from this site. Or he could have forgotten about Mate-matches altogether. She breathed deeply, feeling a wave of relief as she rationalised what must certainly have happened.

Then she froze. There must be some mistake. The profiles showed when a person had last visited the site. And what she saw on the page before her was that he'd visited Mate-matches that day. Not only had he not removed his profile, he was still actively looking.

"Available but choosy!" *Fuck you Art Lionel Brunner!*

She felt the fury burning right through her body. On impulse she started writing an email to him. She told him she thought the actor and writer had done his best work ever. She besieged him with words, questioning how he could have let her enter a field of landmines. And how furious she was with him. So much for "I promise I'll never lie to you"! She wrote for an hour, releasing the full force of her rage.

When she finished she felt better, and then went through her letter, eliminating large chunks of her vitriol, but leaving the parts she still wanted him to read.

She pressed the "send" button, and poured herself another wine. She'd better stop some of this self-medicating. But not now.

Chapter 23

'Our first lunch at the brand new Ricardo's,' said Halle. 'It feels like ages.'

Well, actually, it is,' replied Trudy. It's two months, with the place being closed for refurbishment last month. I've been hanging out for today.'

'Rick must have been thrilled about the opening night. People seemed pretty impressed by the food and the décor,' said Halle.

'And Nina, your painting looks amazing,' added Paula. 'Perfect for the room.'

Nina smiled, almost coyly, a little out of character with her normal rakish manner. 'Must admit I'm pleased with it. My labour of love,' she added with a chuckle. 'Maybe Rick's bringing out a new side of me. Perhaps there's a softer side to this tough old tart that's just been waiting for permission to enter centre stage.' She smiled at them. 'Seriously, though, it was a challenge just because it's so different from my recent paintings.'

'How did you decide on the theme?' asked Trudy.

'Well, actually it came out of a conversation I had with Donna.'

Donna looked puzzled.

'You remember, you talked to me about your visit to Tuscany?'

Donna smiled. 'Yes, I do now. Nina and I were talking about Italy one day, and I was raking up the past. I told her that Martin and I had been to Tuscany for our honeymoon, and how I loved the beauty of the place so much it's been on my wish list ever since.'

'The idea just came out of that conversation. And I enjoyed working in those softer tones. Of course I love that it's looking so good up here. One of the guests at the opening night said she wants to talk about commissioning me to do something for her lounge room. Must say I'm chuffed. I gave her my phone number and I hope she follows up on it. Anyway, most importantly, I love that Rick is so thrilled with it.' Nina had a big grin on her face.

'Talk about the cat that got the cream,' laughed Donna. 'And by the way, you look like you're about fourteen. Love agrees with you.'

'Yeah, I'm feeling like a teenager. I'm wondering what the hell I felt so scared of all this time.' She paused. 'Mind you, I do still occasionally get moments of panic. I want to be with Rick, but I get these rushes of fear, too. It's good to be able to talk to Norm and work through all this old shit in therapy.'

'Yes, I'm pleased you've got him to help you with that,' Donna agreed. She went deep into thought, then added, 'I can tell you, I've needed him this month.'

'Why, what's been happening?' asked Nina.

Donna proceeded to tell them about what had happened with Art.

'The bastard! How can you have been so unlucky again?' asked Nina.

'Well, I was furious. And yes, he is a bastard.' Donna paused. 'But it's actually got me wondering. With a bit of a prod from Trudy.' She smiled wryly. 'I'm the one who's been choosing these guys. I must be doing something wrong. Not picking up on the signs. Or being too trusting too early.' She sat quietly for a moment. 'Norm's been getting to look at my part in the whole sorry sage.'

'Well the next one better scrub up better,' said Paula.

'I think *I* need to be more aware.' Donna was silent again, then added, 'I don't know if I can keep doing this internet thing. But I'll see how I feel down the track. Meanwhile back at the therapy ranch...' She laughed. 'You'd expect by now I'd know more about life. So much for telling me I'd entered the age of wisdom when I turned sixty,' she told Halle. 'Sometimes I reckon I'm still a kindergarten kid in the school of life.'

'But learning all the time. We always do get to know ourselves through our mistakes. Believe me, I certainly have!' offered Trudy.

~~

'This place is packed today,' said Paula. Rick must be feeling pretty good about how Ricardo's is going.'

'He sure is. Most of his established customers have kept coming, and they've been giving him great feedback. He was concerned about going more upmarket, but it's all good.' Nina took a deep breath. 'He's having to work bloody hard, though. And he has his moments of panic, too. The best part is we're able to talk about it all. That's been amazing for me. Apart from you guys I've never had anyone before who understood my meltdowns. He seems to get me.'

'And you get him. Sounds good to me,' said Trudy.

Nina's phone rang. She excused herself and went outside. She returned a couple of minutes later, beaming.

'That's the woman I told you about from the other night. She's asked to see me on Monday to talk about commissioning a painting. How good is that? I'm so used to being a struggling artist, but I'm starting to feel like I've turned a lucky corner.'

'Fantastic. You deserve it. You've worked hard. And Tuscany Dawn is a terrific piece of work. It looks great in the daylight too, by the way. The colours look different than they do at night,' said Donna.

The others chorused their approval.

'Thanks guys.'

'By the way, you're all able to make it to my dinner party next Sunday night?' asked Donna.

'Wouldn't miss it for the world,' answered Trudy. 'It's been too long between dinner parties. You always did it so well.'

'Well, to tell you the truth, I'm pretty nervous about it. Don't remember how to do the hostess thing. Hope I can still cook. I know my food's okay for my family, but then they're family, they'll eat whatever I serve up to them.'

'We promise not to be too critical, even if you serve us up burnt chops,' laughed Paula. 'Anyway, the company's the main thing. We're looking forward to it.'

'Are you asking anyone apart from us?' Halle enquired.

'Don't know. I'm not sure yet.' answered Donna.

'What are you cooking?' asked Nina.

Donna laughed. 'Can't tell. It'll spoil the surprise.' She paused. 'Besides, I haven't actually decided for sure yet. Still looking through my cook books. So it'll be a surprise for me too!'

'You were always a bloody good cook. It can't all have gone down the gurgler,' said Trudy.

'Hope you're right.' Donna smiled. 'I'm hoping it's like riding a bike again. Anyway, even if I am a little bit rusty, I promise I'll get "A" for effort.'

The conversation stopped briefly while lunch came to the table.

'This looks superb,' said Paula. 'Even if it is a salad, it's no ordinary old salad.'

'How's the weight going?' asked Nina. 'You look like you've lost a lot.'

'Yes, five kilos so far. I'm so glad you girls persuaded not to go down the lap-band path. I'm feeling great about it.'

The women all expressed their support, then Halle said, 'You know what, girlfriend. You and I are going on a shopping expedition this week. How are you placed on Tuesday? Time for a complete makeover.'

Paula looked surprised. 'But I don't need any new clothes.'

'Yes you do, you just don't know it.'

'You think so?' She was silent for a moment, then replied, 'Okay, that might be fun.' She started eating the food that had just arrived, and there was a quiet moment while the others began theirs, too.

Nina interrupted the quiet, asking Halle, 'So what's happening with Tilly? Still got the cold war going?'

'Yes, still going at the moment. But I'm not ready to call yet. I'm hoping she'll break the silence.'

'It's about time she came to her senses, isn't it?' snapped Nina.

Halle didn't answer, but Donna noticed her eyes tearing up. 'Leave her alone, Nina. They'll work it out in their own time.'

'It's been going on for bloody years. She's just a spoiled brat,' answered Nina.

Halle stared at her friend. 'You'll see one day it's not so easy when it comes to your own kids.'

Nina was quiet for a moment, then shrugged.

Donna glanced across at Paula, who looked distracted. 'Are you okay?' she asked.

'Yes. I just get a bit sad sometimes when you start talking about kids. It would have been Fran's birthday next week. Ted's coming to the cemetery with me. I'm so grateful to you all, I wouldn't have been able to do it if you hadn't gone to her grave with me a few months back. It's been hard, but I'm coming to terms with it better.' She paused. 'Not that I think I'll ever completely come to terms with it.'

'Well, how could you?' answered Donna, looking fondly at her friend. 'Our kids are such a fundamental part of our lives,' she added, as she slipped into her own thoughts.

Chapter 24

Donna could hear the hum of her friends' voices in the lounge room. She found herself singing as she busied herself with the last of her dinner preparations. Despite all its troughs and peaks, overall she had an increasing sense of contentment in her day-to-day life. Like an explorer traversing unknown territory, she was starting to feel more familiar with the terrain.

She finished blending the pea and asparagus soup she'd cooked for her friends, who were happily chatting over drinks and dips. She placed the blended mixture back in the saucepan to reheat at the last minute, and took the sour cream out of the fridge, ready to add to the soup once she dished it up.

Not wanting to be away from her guests for too long, she walked back into the lounge room. After some deliberation, she had decided to invite Murray to come tonight. She'd talked it over with Trudy, who'd agreed with her that since she'd been honest with him about the shape of their relationship it would be good to invite him, as a friend, to join them. He fitted in well. He and Alan seemed to have a good rapport. Alan had discovered Murray's association with literature, and they were engrossed in conversation about some of their favourite authors.

It was such a pity, she thought. That magic ingredient. Could she accommodate the lack of it? Would it come with time? Then she decided she didn't need to worry about that now. Just enjoy the night with her closest and dearest friends.

It was good to see Nina looking so happy. Since it was Sunday and Ricardo's didn't open tonight, Rick had been able to come to the dinner. It felt a little strange to see him out of context, but Donna was thrilled to be able to have him here with their friend.

They looked good together, she thought. About time. She'd hated seeing Nina in that go-nowhere situation with Tony.

'How long have you been running the restaurant?' Murray asked Rick.

'About five years. Rick's Café was a huge first step for me,' he said. 'I'd only been a home cook before that, although it was my passion. I've wanted to do the changes for so long, in fact it was my vision when I first opened the café, but I couldn't afford it at the time. And it's better now, anyway, because I've had more experience and I've got a loyal clientele who've given me lots of encouragement. So the bigger dream...to be able to transform it into Ricardo's...well, there are moments when it feels like it's just a dream and I'm going to wake up. Not bad for the boy from Sunshine, hey? And having this young woman in my life is feeling pretty damn amazing, too.' He drew Nina closer to him.

'Now all you need is a Tattslotto win and you'll have the hat-trick,' laughed Halle.

'Life's already about as rich as I could ever have wished. Just keep your fingers crossed for me that the restaurant goes well.'

'We'll have to go there for dinner soon,' added Ted. 'Paula has been telling me about your new menu. And now that you're also opening at night I'm keen to try it out for myself.'

'I'll look forward to seeing you here,' answered Rick.

'Nina, Donna mentioned to me that someone was interested in you doing a painting for them,' said Murray. 'How did your meeting with her go?'

'Fantastic. She wants a large painting, about two metres square, to go on her living room wall.'

'Has she said much about what she's wanting you to do?' asked Trudy.

'Yes, a bit. It's a modern house, you know that minimalist look, so it'll need to be quite different to Tuscany Dawn. To tell you the truth I was surprised she asked me because what she wants *is* so different to Rick's painting. But she said she saw my work at that exhibition I had last year. And this'll actually be similar to my usual style. We're still discussing the theme and colours.'

'What a great break for you, said Paula.

'Yes, I'm so excited about it. She wants the painting to be a real stand-out feature. And she intimated to me that she has important friends who'll see it. I think that's just her way of keeping me on my toes. Not that I'm needing a prod. I'll put my heart and soul into it. Always do.'

'Hope you're still going to want to come to our lunches when you're a famous artist,' laughed Trudy.

'Just try and keep me away.'

Donna interrupted the conversation to say that dinner was ready and got everyone seated at the table. 'You know this is my first dinner party for years, so here goes,' she said, a slightly nervous tone to her voice.

Donna served the soup. It felt good to be playing hostess again. After all this time she'd almost forgotten how much she enjoyed it.

'I'll have to find out how to do this soup for the restaurant,' laughed Rick. 'It's great.'

Donna felt radiant. Life was good. She almost felt like the Donna of old. But with an added dimension. She was learning a lot about living. And for the first time she could appreciate the time she'd spent alone after her divorce. She smiled to herself. The evolution of Donna Quixote.

~~

'That was a thoroughly enjoyable night. Thank you so much for inviting me.'

Murray had insisted on helping her tidy and clear the dishes when the others left.

'You and Alan seemed to have a lot to talk about.'

'Yes, we share a love of literature. And as we talked it turned out that we'd met before. It was a long time ago, probably ten years. We had a mutual friend, and our paths crossed through him. Thank you for tonight. It was a terrific night. The food was delicious. And you've got lovely friends.'

'Yes. I don't know what I would have done without them.'

They were silent for a moment, with just the sound of Eric Clapton playing in the background. Tears in Heaven. That song always got to her.

'I'm pleased we've met. We can have a good friendship. Unless you've changed your mind, that is,' Murray said, laughing.

'Good friendship sounds perfect.'

'So how about we catch a movie next week.'

'What will we go to see?'

They chatted for the next hour while he helped her with the dishes, then gave her a gentle kiss on the cheek before leaving. She was grateful again that he was a gentleman.

~~

'Great dinner party, Donna,' said Halle. The women were engrossed in their usual "post-mortem" of events over lunch. 'The food was superb. No need for you to have been worried. I'm putting in my order for more of the same. And Sophia asked me get the recipe for that delicious lamb dish. Unless it's one of those old family secrets you can't give away.'

Donna laughed. 'I'll give it to you with pleasure. I thought I might have forgotten how to do it, but I loved playing hostess. So there'll be no stopping me now.'

'Murray seems a nice guy,' said Paula.

'Yes, he is a terrific guy. It feels like we'll be good friends. Just friends.'

'Anyone else on the scene?' asked Halle.

'Not at the moment. A couple of guys that I'm talking with by email. But no-one I'm enthusiastic about. I wasn't sure if I'd go back to the online thing, but decided I'd give it another go. And by the way, I noticed Harvey is back online.'

'The bastard! Fishing for some other poor woman to take the hook.' Trudy was furious.

'Yes. I've been considering writing to One Plus One and voicing my concerns. The man obviously has no conscience.' Donna almost hissed the words. 'I still can't believe that I actually fell for his bloody sociopathic charm. And then getting sucked in by Art!'

'Well, I doubt anyone will get past you so easily again,' said Halle.

'Well, I sure hope I've learned something this time around!'

'Talk about learning lessons, that altercation I had with Tilly seems to have worked wonders. She's got herself a job. Working in a book shop. And we're talking again and back on track, thank goodness.' Halle looked relieved.

'That's good news. For you and for her,' said Donna.

'Yes. I know I should have stopped supporting her a long time ago. I just didn't seem to be able to do it. It took all of you belting me around the ears to get to the stage where I just had to draw that line in the sand. And there was too much at stake when she started challenging my relationship with Sophia. If it had been less important I might have succumbed to her manipulation. Anyway, it's done.'

'Thank God for that,' said Nina.

'And how is she now about Sophia?' asked Paula.

'We've had to wave the white flag on that one for the time being. I'm hoping she'll come to her senses eventually, because that's not going to change. I hope she's starting to get to understand that now.'

There was a temporary lull in the conversation, as lunch arrived. A bottle of Chilean wine accompanied their meal, courtesy of Rick.

'We're going to be drinking the profits,' said Halle. 'That's lovely of him.'

Everyone busied themselves with tasting their lunch choices.

Then Nina said, 'By the way, I'm going to meet David, Rick's son, next week.'

'How are you feeling about it? Last time we spoke about it you were nervous at the thought,' said Donna.

'I'm still anxious. Not about the "commitment" part of it. Strangely enough, I'm less afraid of that now. I feel like we're actually a couple. Real grown ups.' She laughed. Then she added, 'It's more about how David and I will get on. Will he like me? And will I know how to be with him. I don't know much about how to talk to kids, you know.'

'How old is he?' asked Trudy.

'He's nine. He looks like a beautiful kid. He looks just like his Dad, actually. But what if he hates me?' She laughed. 'Listen to me! When did you ever hear me worried about whether someone would like me?'

'Just be yourself. He'll love you,' answered Donna. 'And don't try to rush the relationship with him. There's plenty of time for the two of you to get to know each other.'

Nina nodded, but didn't reply. Donna watched her, smiling to herself to see the softening of her usually outrageously flamboyant friend. Nina was probably right: finding love seemed to be ushering in the more tender, sensitive side of her personality. Donna felt a wave of warmth towards her, and empathy for the vulnerability that she saw. We all have our vulnerable moments, she thought. She drifted off onto her own tangent.

Trudy raised her eyebrows. 'What happened to you then? Something on your mind?' she asked Donna.

'Hm. Yeah. I was talking to Becky this morning. She hinted that she and James were feeling concerned about Luke. She wouldn't elaborate, and I don't know what's going on. I've been a bit concerned myself, to tell you the truth. He hasn't been writing to me, and he used to call me every week, but I'm finding his calls are less and less frequent. Sometimes I've wondered about how good his relationship with Jacquie is. I feel like there's been some tension there lately, but I haven't wanted to be one of those interfering mums.' She was quiet. 'I'm seeing Becky in the morning, so maybe she'll say more then. Or maybe I'll risk being an interfering mother and just try to phone Luke again and ask him what's going on.' She paused. 'I don't know what, but I know there's something up.' She sighed. 'Time to get the bill?'

Chapter 25

Donna was back at her favourite Saturday morning cafe, the familiar untidy spread of newspaper on the table in front of her. It was cold outside, and she could hear the sound of rain on the roof. But it was cosy and warm inside, and she was enjoying a peaceful, almost meditative state, as she sat staring into the log fire flames. There was something hypnotic about fire. Fire and water often affected her like this. The natural elements. It must be something primal, she decided.

'Hi.'

She jumped, jolted out of her reverie. It was that guy she'd seen here before. 'Hello,' she replied.

'Looks like you're a Saturday morning regular, too. Good coffee, hey?'

'Yes. The food's not bad, either.' She smiled.

'I'm Patrick, by the way.'

'Donna.'

They chatted for a couple more minutes, then he said, 'Enjoy your breakfast. Or is it lunch?' He smiled, and with a nod made his way over to the same table in the corner she'd seen him at previously.'

He was an attractive looking guy. Green eyes. Dark, curly hair. Donna noticed a slight increase in her heartbeat, then deliberately shifted her attention back to her Sudoku puzzle.

~~

Half an hour had passed, and Donna was feeling frustrated. Her Sudoku wasn't working. Some silly little slip somewhere had thrown the whole thing out. She must photo-copy it in future, she told herself. At least then she could start afresh on a clean copy if this happened.

She glanced up, and caught Patrick looking at her. He smiled at her, and after returning the gesture she went back to erasing the first segment of her puzzle. She'd found herself glancing across at him much too often. Like a silly school-girl, she decided, determined to bring herself back into line.

~ ~

'Donna? I hope I'm not being intrusive, I can see you're busy there with that damn frustrating Sudoku. I'm quite addicted to them myself, I must admit. But I just wondered if you'd like to have a coffee with me?' Then he added, ' Hope I'm not being too pushy.'

He had a slightly lopsided smile, she noticed now. Almost a shyness about him. But not too shy, she decided. Here he was inviting her to have a coffee with him.

'Yes, that would be good,' she answered, aware again that her heart was thumping. It felt so loud in her chest she fantasised for a moment that he must be able to hear it pounding against her chest wall.

'Your table or mine?' he grinned.

'Well, if you don't mind the newspaper tablecloth you might as well stay here.'

He sat down, and signaled the passing waitress to catch her attention, then checking what she wanted to drink ordered two lattes.

'Unless you'd like something stronger,' he laughed.

'Too early in the day for me.'

They sat sipping their coffee, going through that process of two strangers getting to know each other. She found out he had three children, two married, the other a dedicated career hound.

143

'I don't know that she's anywhere near ready to settle down yet. I hope she doesn't leave it too late, and then suddenly wonders where the hell the years went,' he said.

Donna noticed he looked sad, but decided not to comment. A short silence was broken by the arrival of their coffee.

'We're lucky we get good coffee here,' Patrick commented. 'I just got back from the U.S. a couple of weeks ago. I found I was hanging out for a Coffee Pot latte. Didn't get one there as good as this.'

'Have you done much travelling?'

'Yes, quite a lot. I spent a few months in Europe last year. I did a couple of "gourmet walking tours".'

'Sounds like an eat fest,' laughed Donna.

'Yes. The last one I did was in Italy. It was beautiful. We started in Torina, and worked our way through Piedmont. Then Cinque Terre. Have you been there?'

'No. I've been to Italy, but not there. That's those little fishing villages, isn't it?'

'Yeah. Quite idyllic. The walking track there went through the Cinque Terre National Park. Loved it. I hope to get back there some time.'

'Sounds wonderful. What about the food?'

'The food was great. We had great gourmet meals along the way. And I met some interesting people in the group from all over the world. We've kept contact. You know, we all hope we'll cross paths or visit each other again. I don't know if that will happen, but I hope if they ever got to Oz they would look me up.'

'So would you do more of those tours?'

'Yeah. I'm thinking about doing another one next year. But I like to get away and walk on my own sometimes, too. Lots of time for personal reflection. You know, sorting out bits of your life that often get neglected by busy-ness.' He was quiet for a moment, before continuing, 'I might even do a tour of the crop circles in the

U.K one day, and look around the country. Have you heard about crop circles?'

'Yes, a bit.'

'I'm undecided about them. I'm stuck between being a complete skeptic and quite curious.'

'Fascinating.'

'Yeah. So many places I'd like to see. But I've done nothing but talk about me. What about you? Done any travelling?'

'Yes, some. Feels like an eternity ago, though. I've been to Spain. And I was in Tuscany. For my honeymoon.'

'Magical, isn't it?'

Donna nodded. She told him about a couple of the trips she and Martin had done all those years ago. 'Maybe I'll do some more one day, who knows?'

'I've been writing about mine. A sort of fictional account that just started off as a journal but grew. That's one of the things I love to do here. Just sit at my table in the corner and write. And every now and then I spread out my photos on my dining room table at home and get some more inspiration for the lives of my characters. Maybe you'd like to see my photos some time?'

'I'd love to.'

Patrick laughed. 'My God, I hope that didn't sound like a terrible pick-up line. "Come up and see my photos some time". But I thought you might enjoy them. Maybe I could bring some here one day for you to see.'

Donna laughed too, noting how his face lit up when as he talked about his travels and his writing. And he looked great when he laughed.

She found out he was an accountant.

'But please don't hold that against me. Hopefully I'm not one of those boring ones who make a habit of always dotting all the i's and crossing the t's. Accounting is my work, not my life.'

Donna smiled. She already had a sense that he was anything but boring.

They chatted with a comfortable easiness. They were on their second cup of coffee when he said, 'This feels good. Well, I don't know about you but I'm enjoying myself.'

'Are you now?' She smiled at him.

'Yeah. But I've been keeping an eye on you for a long time, you know. It's taken me months to pluck up the courage to do this.'

'Really?' Her eyebrows were raised in genuine astonishment.

'Uh-huh. You seem surprised.' Then, 'You didn't notice me noticing you?'

'No…not before last time we spoke here.'

'So…I've seen that you've usually been here alone or meeting a woman friend. I'm hoping that means you're single?'

'Yes. And you?'

'Yeah. Been on my own for a couple of years now. Bad marriage. Second time round, too. Not exactly a perfect relationship history. Got it wrong both times.' He smiled a wry smile. 'Pretty poor advertisement, I suppose.'

Donna had memories of Martin and Harvey and Art running through her brain. Like the frames of a movie, sometimes fast, at other moments freezing on some of the more painful frames. Her track record wasn't so good either. She looked directly into Patrick's eyes, an unasked question like a thread between them.

'They both cheated on me. Bad choices. That's my failing, I haven't chosen well. Not what I thought I was signing up for, either time.'

Donna saw a glance of pain cross his face.

'What about you?'

'One marriage. Similar story to yours. You know, the typical tale. Left me for a younger woman. Then after that I had no-one for eight years, I didn't feel brave enough to try again. One brief relationship a few months back…a bad choice. Then another disaster.' She smiled wryly. 'Talk about "come in spinner". The first one was married, but told me they lived together but were separated. The second one wasn't much better. Totally fooled me.

146

For a little while I beat myself up for not being able to pick up the signs.' She paused. She took another sip of her coffee. 'Hey, listen to us. I don't think we're supposed to talk about our past relationships on a first date.' Then she grinned. 'Is this a date?'

'We can call it whatever you like,' he said, smiling.

He had an open face. She was enjoying herself.

Patrick glanced at his watch. 'I'm going to have to go in a minute. I've arranged to go over and help my youngest daughter with some bits and pieces around the house.' He hesitated, then asked, 'How would you like to have dinner with me one night?'

'Sounds good. I'd love to do that.'

He put on a dark green jacket that he'd thrown across the back of the chair, and a striped scarf.

'It's pretty cold outside. Much nicer with that fire going in here. Wish I didn't have to go now.'

They exchanged phone numbers, and before she knew it he'd gone, waving as he left the café. She felt warm. She knew it was not just from the fire. She folded her newspaper and went to pay for her breakfast but found that Patrick had already settled the bill. She wondered when he'd call her. Soon, she hoped.

Chapter Twenty-six

'How did your meeting with Rick's son go?' Paula looked keenly at Nina, waiting to hear what had happened since their last lunch.

'Actually, much better than I expected. The first ten or fifteen minutes felt odd; we were both as nervous as each other. But Rick was good, he kept things going until we both felt more at ease. And I remembered Rick had told me David was a big Star Wars fan. I asked him a question about that and it was like a magic door opened. There was no stopping him once that happened. And he's a nice kid. By the end of the afternoon he was asking when we could catch up again. Big relief. And Rick was thrilled. Although he said to me he hadn't been too worried that we'd hit it off.'

'What about your painting? Any advancement on last time?' asked Trudy.

'Yes, I've had a few ideas, and I'm playing around with them at the moment.'

'And what's happening with you, Donna? Have you seen Murray at all? Any further developments?' asked Paula. 'Or any other guys from One Plus One breaking down your door?'

'Yes to the first and no to the second. Murray and I went to see a film last week, and we had coffee one evening. Great guy. But still just a friend. It'll never be anything else. And I still get the occasional "hug" from someone online, but there's been no-one of interest there.' She paused, then continued, 'But I am going out to dinner with someone this week.'

'What? Where did you find him? Who's this mystery stranger? Come on, fill us in on the details. You know we're your committee,' said Halle. 'We let a couple get past us, but that's not going to happen again.'

'His name's Patrick.' She told her friends about their meeting. 'Actually, Trudy, you might have even seen him at The Coffee Pot when we've caught up there. He's a regular on Saturdays, too. Anyway, he's very interesting. And he does seem to make this old heart of mine flutter.'

'I told you there was still life in the old girl,' laughed Trudy. 'You're nowhere near ready to shut shop yet. You can't keep a good gal down for long. You've only just begun.'

Donna smiled. 'Who would have believed all this a few years back? I thought things could never be good again. It seems unbelievable now how hopeless I felt. But I must say that I'm enjoying my life. Even the glitches like the Harvey and Art episodes. I've actually felt stronger since then.'

'Can't wait to hear the next chapter,' said Nina. 'Now that I'm hooked up with Rick and Halle's got Sophia we're depending on you to provide the dating spice to our lunches.'

Donna laughed. 'Well, I hope I can keep you entertained.'

'It's good for me to be able to live vicariously' sighed Trudy. God knows I need it sometimes. I need something to add some spice to *my* life. Just don't know what it is I want.' I've been going to some U3A courses, but they just don't seem to fill the gap. I've got to say I've been feeing pretty empty for a while now.'

'What about going back to do some more formal study? I bet you'd enjoy it, suggested Halle.'

Trudy was silent for a while, then said, 'You mean some university course?'

Halle nodded.

'I don't know if I could do it. It's been so long since I disciplined myself to do anything like that. I don't know if I'm capable of studying at Uni level.'

'Bullshit, Trudy,' said Nina. 'That's just not true.'

'I don't know what I'd do.'

'Just depends on what excites you. It's not like you have to worry about a career later. You'd be doing it more for the love of it.'

Trudy didn't answer for a while. After a couple of minutes she said, 'You know, I actually wouldn't mind considering it. I've always had an interest in history. And literature. Maybe I could get my brain going again. I'll have a chat to Alan and think some more about it.' She paused. 'Anyway, we moved away from this man you were talking about, Donna. I want to hear more. We don't want you jumping in without caution this time! How old is he? Been married? Children? What sort of work does he do?'

'Talk about twenty questions,' chuckled Donna, who proceeded to answer what she knew. 'But I'm only just getting to know the guy. Anyway, I like him and actually feel quite excited about seeing him again. That's a pretty good start. Next installment coming up. God, I'm starting to feel like Days of Our Lives.'

Changing the subject, she turned to Paula. 'I was concerned about you during the week. How did you pull up after the cemetery?'

'Cried my eyes out. More than I've ever cried in my life. I kept feeling there couldn't be any more tears but they just kept coming. Ted was a wonderful support. And you know, I've been feeling better since then. Apart from that day when you all were there with me at Fran's grave I haven't done much crying. But I've needed the release.'

'Yeah, it's how we heal,' Trudy said. 'I remember when Alan's brother died a couple of years back he bottled it up…probably for about a year. Benny was his "baby" brother, fifteen years younger, and he'd always been a bit of a second dad to him. Then one night we were watching some movie, just an ordinary movie with a fairly ordinary scene, but something triggered him and he just started sobbing non-stop. He said after he realised he'd been holding it in and just trying to soldier on, but it was a volcano waiting to erupt. He felt so much better after that. too.'

Paula nodded. 'Yes, I know I've been doing that for too long. And I'm sure putting on all that weight was tied up in my grief. Instead of letting it all out I just ate. Mood food. Keeping the feelings at bay. And I can see that I'm not doing that so much recently.'

Donna found herself trying to remember what had happened when Martin left her. How much had she cried? She recalled feeling a numb disbelief. Raw, frozen. At least in the beginning. She sighed, but it was a sigh of relief. She had difficulty now recognising how she'd felt despairing enough to want to end her life. She felt sorry for people who didn't have the sorts of supports she'd had.

She found herself thinking more about Patrick. She didn't want to jump too far ahead. And she certainly didn't want another catastrophe like the Harvey and Art debacles. She was enjoying the excited buzz of anticipation, but… little baby steps, important to just take it slowly, she reminded herself. Yet she had a good feeling about this one.

She shifted her mind to the other pressing issue for her right now. 'Luke's back in Melbourne.'

'When did he get back?' asked Paula.

'He got back a few days ago. I'm catching up with him tomorrow morning. He's kept putting it off for a couple of days.' Donna was thoughtful. 'I've barely heard from him over the last few months. That's unusual. He seemed like he didn't want to come tomorrow, but I kept pushing it. Which confirms for me that there's something going on that he's reluctant to talk about. But in the end he agreed to come round and have breakfast with me.'

'So how are you feeling about it?' asked Halle.

'Concerned. He was always so open with me, but I've noticed how much he's drawn back. Actually, the more I think about it, it's been a gradual withdrawal over the last couple of years. And I've been hurt. I don't understand it. We were always so close. I keep asking myself why the moving away. As far as I know I haven't done anything wrong. But you know how you question yourself? Anyway, hopefully I'll know more tomorrow.'

'Well, give me a call if you feel like a coffee and chat afterwards,' said Trudy.

'Thanks, Trude. I may do that.

Nina interrupted the conversation. 'I'm off now. I've got a couple of messages to do…and a painting to work on. I've had a couple of ideas while we've been talking this afternoon that I want to sketch. So see you next month.'

Chapter 27

Donna had trouble getting out of bed. It had been a long time since she'd felt like this. Surprising, especially with Luke coming over. But she had a bad feeling about this morning. The more she thought about it the more she realised how long it had been since he'd had a conversation with her. A personal conversation, anyway.

The phone rang as she got the croissants ready to put into the oven. She hoped it wasn't him phoning to cancel.

'Hi Mum. I've been held up.'

'You're still coming, though?'

There was silence at the other end of the phone. She could hear him breathe deeply, then he sighed. 'I'll be there. It'll be about another hour.'

'See you then.'

Donna poured herself a coffee, and tried to read the morning paper. But she found herself re-reading the same paragraph over and over. Something just didn't feel right. This wasn't her Luke.

~~

The doorbell rang. Once. Then again, as if impatiently. She walked briskly to open the front door.

'Hi, darling.'

'Hi Mum.'

'Are you okay?'

He didn't look okay. Red-rimmed eyes. And something else she couldn't quite define. Donna leaned forward to kiss him. Alcohol. He was reeking of alcohol. She stepped back, alarmed. Heavy night? Or had he been drinking already this morning?

'Come in. It's so good to see you. I've missed you, darling.'

'Yeah.'

His eyes were averted. Something was definitely amiss. They'd always been so close, but now she could feel a wall between them. He walked slowly, unsteady on his feet, and followed her into the lounge room.

'I've got some croissants that'll be ready in a minute. Do you want a coffee?'

'Thanks, Mum. Nothing to eat; but coffee would be great. I can't stay long. I just wanted to say hello, but I've got to go and see someone.'

Donna felt a knot in her stomach. Her mind was racing as she went to boil the kettle. Should she ask him if he'd been drinking? (He obviously had!) Or would he get angry with her if she did? Did it matter if he did get angry? What was wrong? The uneasiness that she felt, the queasiness in her stomach, fitted with the sense she'd had for a while that things were not okay.

She poured the coffee, and took the two cups into the other room where he was slumped on the couch.

'Luke, what's happening there? You're not yourself.' Let him tell her without her having to pry for answers.

'Just feeling jetlagged.'

'Hon…you've been drinking.'

Luke was silent. His eyes were ablaze now. Donna felt nauseous. 'No.'

Why was he lying to her? This was not the Luke she knew. No point pushing, though. He had a look on her face that said "leave me alone".

He finished his coffee, making vague attempts at small talk, but drying up almost as quickly as he spoke, then got up hurriedly.

'Sorry, Mum. I have to go now.'

He was out the door with an unconvincing assurance that they'd get together soon. 'As soon as I'm over this jetlag.'

~~

Donna felt breathless. Her heart was thumping. Take it easy, she urged herself. She took a few deep breaths like Norm had taught her to do when she was stressed. After a few minutes she could feel herself relax a little.

She walked to the phone and dialled Martin's number, feeling a little shaky. It must be five years since they'd had any contact at all. But this felt critical. And maybe he knew what was going on.

'Hello Martin.'

A pause at the other end of the phone. 'Hello.'

She thought she heard a quiver in his voice. That voice that she used to know so well.

'I…I just wondered if you've had contact with Luke, and if you know what's going on. I know something's up. I know things aren't okay.'

'Yeah.' He hesitated. 'Look, how about we have a cuppa and I'll fill you in on what I know.'

'Okay. Why don't you come over here? I need you to tell me.'

'Be there in half an hour.'

~~

It felt strange to be sitting opposite him. All the years of familiarity, and then the long estrangement. He'd aged a lot. And lost weight since she'd seen him. In spite of herself Donna felt a protective warmth towards him. For a while the hurt and disappointment were replaced with more tender feelings. All the years they'd spent with each other came together in the moment. And he was looking at her with the same nostalgic affection.

'I'm so sorry, Donna. I wish I hadn't hurt you.'

She sat without answering. She didn't want to get too caught up in anything about them. This was about Luke.

She didn't respond to his apology. 'What do you know about what's going on with Luke? He turned up this morning reeking of

155

alcohol, and it's felt like he hasn't been himself for a long time. He wouldn't talk to me this morning.'

Martin nodded. 'Yeah. He contacted me a couple of weeks ago. He made me promise not to say anything to you. He didn't want to worry you. And he's feeling ashamed. Donna, I paid for him to come over here. He needs us both. Things have gone completely pear-shaped for him back in London. He lost his job. And Jacquie kicked him out.' He paused. 'He's got a drinking problem. It took him a while to admit it, but the shit seriously hit the fan back home. He was distraught when he phoned me. I'd been wondering about contacting you. We need to talk to him. Together, if you'll agree to it. I've been making some enquiries about rehab. We need to show some combined support.'

Donna felt her stomach lurch. She thought she was going to be sick. She wiped her brow. She needed some cold water on her face, which was burning. She ran into the bathroom. Martin followed her, a concerned look on his face.

'Hey, are you okay?'

'I'm just a bit overwhelmed. Although I knew something was wrong it's hit me pretty hard.'

Martin came up close behind her and put his arm around her shoulders. Neither of them spoke for a while. Then he said, 'How about I make you a cup of coffee?'

She smiled weakly. 'Okay. That'd be good.'

He looked at her. 'Still white with one sugar?'

She nodded. It felt good that he remembered. 'Thanks, Marty.' She was aware she'd called him by his old familiar name.

He squeezed her shoulder before walking away to make the coffee. Donna reflected on what she was coming to understand. Her panic was subsiding now. The fear. But she felt hurt, too. How come Luke hadn't been able to talk to her? She'd always believed they were so close. How come he'd called Martin and not her? She remembered what Martin had said. Luke had wanted to protect her. It still hurt, though.

After a moment she washed her face, took a deep breath and walked back into the lounge room. This was about Luke, she reminded herself again. Never mind her wounded pride. She needed to be strong for him. 'Okay. How do you suggest we go about doing this?'

Martin handed her the coffee he'd made, and took out a notepad. She suddenly felt calmer. It felt good to have him take over. She'd forgotten what it was like to let him be in charge. She'd been the one to organise the social aspects of their life. But it had always been Martin who'd made all the big decisions and handled whatever crises came up. And she'd lost sight of the feeling of being able to rely on him. Completely rely on him. He'd been the rock. She knew now he'd handle it.

But she also knew this was going to take two of them. And she was aware now she could be part of helping Luke in whatever way he needed. After all these years, and after everything that had gone on between them, she and Martin were going to be able to unite as a team and support Luke through his difficulties.

'I'm glad you're here. We can work together in this.'

Martin nodded. His eyes looked straight into hers. She'd forgotten how blue they were. She'd forgotten that look.

'Okay. I've been making enquiries.' He looked at the notepad, and handed it to her. 'These are the rehab places I've found. And I spoke to Doctor Brooks about it. This is how I think we need to go about it. I'll ask Luke to come over here tomorrow night if that's okay with you?'

Donna sighed. This was not going to be easy.

Chapter 28

Donna put the finishing touches to her make-up. Patrick was due in another fifteen minutes. She wasn't sure if she felt like going tonight. Not that she didn't want to see Patrick. In fact she'd been keen to get his call. It was just that her mind was caught up in the events of the past couple of days. It was so hard to see her thirty-two year old son in crisis.

~~

At first Luke had been defensive, denying the severity of what was happening in his life. 'Jacquie and I have been through a rough patch. Nothing we can't work out, though.'

Donna looked at Martin, waiting to see how he'd handle this.

'Why do you think she left you?' he asked.

'Just a couple of things we need to work through.'

'And your work? What was that about?'

'I didn't get on well with the CEO.'

Martin didn't answer immediately, then he looked Luke directly in the eyes. He averted his face, breaking eye contact.

'Luke, we need to get honest here. Cut out the bullshit. This isn't what you told me on the phone. Your Mum and I both know what's going on. You've got a problem. You're drinking.'

'Yeah, I have a bit. It's been my way of dealing with the stuff that's been happening.'

Martin didn't answer, but again looked straight at him.

Luke suddenly started sobbing, startling Donna. He sobbed so hard he could hardly get the words out.

'I'm…I'm sorry, Mum. Sorry, Dad. I hate letting you both down. I've felt so stuck.'

He looked more like the little ten-year-old they'd reared together, his adulthood temporarily drowned by vulnerability and tears. Donna put her arm around Luke's shoulders.

When the sobbing subsided, Martin spoke clearly and firmly. 'You need help for your alcoholism, son.'

There. He'd named it. And Luke had blinked, but just nodded. Donna had thought he even looked relieved. Out in the open. With the two people that he knew would accept him through whatever it took.

Donna's chest had felt like it could explode as she heard Martin talk about rehab options. He'd systematically researched it all. Thank God he'd taken control. Now it needed Luke to step up and do what was necessary. Her heart was thumping so hard it almost hurt. The only thing she could think to say for now was, 'You know we're here for you, darling. We'll always be here.'

Slide shots in her mind. Luke's first steps. Starting school. His first blue ribbon that he'd proudly displayed when he won his third grade race. Dux of his school. Graduation from Uni. Starting his career in Law. The job in London. He'd excelled in whatever he took on. A perfect prelude to the rest of his life. Now he looked pathetic. Life gone wrong. The performance hadn't lived up to the dress rehearsal. How had this happened?

'I know Mum', he said, as if reading her mind. 'I've completely stuffed things up.'

Just get in there and fix it. Get back to being my Luke. Take this pain away. Donna blinked, feeling guilty; she reminded herself to stop feeling sorry for herself. This was not about her.

~~

She slipped into her zebra-striped pants. Still looking okay there, she reassured herself. The doorbell rang. God, she'd lost track of time! First time she remembered that happening. Ms Punctuality, late? Maybe she was getting over her obsession with time.

Walking downstairs towards the front door, her mind relived her conversation with Trudy a few days back. Although she'd been hurt by her friend's words, Donna knew she'd been right about her crazy fling with Art. She had to admit to herself that she *had* ignored the signals. First with Harvey. Then Art. And now? *Three strikes and you're out.*

How could she have been so foolish? Easy to see in hindsight, of course. But then as Norm often reminded her, insights always initially emerge in hindsight. No point in beating herself up. As long as she didn't make the same mistakes again.

But now she was about to have dinner with another man. And what did she know about Patrick? Next to nothing. Foot on brake, girl, she reminded herself as she went to open the door.

A dark navy jacket over a grey polo neck, and a scarf nonchalantly thrown around his neck. He looked great! But then a warning bell on the edge of her brain, disturbing the slight excitement that threatened to overtake her senses: don't get too caught up there. You've had enough disasters to last a lifetime. And now she could hear Norm's words of wisdom in her head, in a race with the euphoria, with Trudy's advice running a close third.

Patrick smiled, and the race was temporarily dismissed from her brain.

'Hi. Come in.'

He had that slightly shy-looking grin again that she'd seen and found endearing at the café that day.

'Would you like a drink?'

'Thanks, but I'll wait till we get to the restaurant. I've booked for seven thirty. How about we make our way there and have a drink there? I've got a nice bottle of Shiraz in the car. I hope that's okay? Otherwise I'll order a bottle at the restaurant.'

'No, sounds good. Shiraz's my drink.' She smiled.

Donna closed the front door behind them and walked with him to his car, a buzz of excitement spoiled only slightly by the anxious knot in her stomach.

~~

Donna sat quietly, sipping the remains of her coffee. It was cold. Patrick had left five minutes ago, and she was reflecting on the evening. They'd eaten at a lovely French restaurant she'd never been to before, and their conversation had flowed easily throughout the meal. She'd heard more about him: about his family when they moved to Australia from Seattle when he was two years old, his parents' shock divorce when he was just twelve, and his own marriage disasters. She told him more about her life, and even found herself confiding in him about the recent events with Luke.

She told herself it was quite different to what she had experienced previously with either Harvey or with Art. Or was she fooling herself? Because that's what she'd thought about them, too. She tried to fathom what felt different. She had a strong sense of being heard, she decided, and an openness in Patrick that she hoped was genuine. Not that there wasn't a strong attraction. That was there, all right. In fact when they came back to her place for coffee she had to admit she was disappointed he'd been such a gentleman. And when he'd said goodnight he'd just given her a kiss on the cheek. Perhaps she didn't appeal to him? Perhaps he felt like she'd felt with Murray? A friendship, but nothing more.

Her thoughts tumbled rapidly now as she sat in the dim light of her lounge-room, immersed in her post-evening appraisal, trying to make sense of her feelings. Ridiculous. She felt like a sixty-year-old adolescent!

Then a sinking feeling hurtled into her psyche again as she thought about the situation with Luke. Probably the last thing she needed now was to get caught up in another relationship, anyway.

She was going to need to be available for Luke. He was going to need every bit of support she and Martin could give him.

She suddenly felt sick. How could she have enjoyed herself like that? How could she let herself get so caught up in Patrick? What sort of mother was she?

Maybe she just needed some distraction from the panicky feelings for a while. She started to pour herself a wine, then stopped herself with a jolt. Perhaps this was how Luke started his downslide. Just another drink to blur his confusion or pain. Then another. She sat staring into space before the tears started to cascade down her face.

Chapter 29

Donna walked towards the phone as it continued to puncture the silence with its harsh ringtone. She was numb. How could she feel numbness and pain at the same time?

Yesterday she and Martin had driven Luke to rehab. She could hardly bear to see her boy's forlorn, anxiety-racked eyes. At first he'd been angry with them and adamant he didn't need to go. But as they got ready to leave him he'd turned to them both.

'I'll make it up to you both, I promise.'

Pathetic. And so sad. The ten-year-old boy again, in a man's body.

'Do this for yourself, son. We love you, but you know you need to be doing this for yourself,' Martin had answered.

Donna had looked at Martin as he spoke. Again she'd felt comforted knowing she could rely on his rock-solid control of the situation. Would she have been able to manage if he'd not taken over? But she knew she would have somehow gathered the strength, because Luke was her boy, and he needed her. For now, though, all the emotional fortitude she thought she'd developed over recent years felt eroded, so she'd been grateful Martin was there. She'd looked again at him and felt a surge of warmth, probably a vestige of the affection she'd felt for him during all their years together.

Reflecting on that now she was surprised she'd felt tenderness after all the years of rage and hurt she'd struggled with. Perhaps the past could finally be left behind.

The phone's ring was persistent. She picked it up, hearing her own weary voice say, 'Hello'.

'Hi Donna. Just calling to see how you're doing.'

It was Patrick. He'd called the previous night to ask if she'd like to catch a movie together. She'd put him off. She couldn't find the energy to see him. The last thing she wanted right now was another man messing up her life. *God, where did that come from?* She sounded bitter. Just a passing mood, she assured herself. She simply wasn't up to opening herself to more vulnerability at the moment.

She'd already brought Patrick up to date the night before about what was happening with Luke. 'So I hope you understand. I'm just not in a space to be able to give you anything at all now,' she'd said, aware as she spoke of the slight abrasive edge to her voice; but she hadn't been able to muster anything more friendly.

That was just yesterday, so she hadn't expected to hear from him so soon. If ever. She certainly hadn't been welcoming. Probably even rude, if she was honest with herself.

She hesitated now at the sound of his voice. He sounded quite concerned.

'I'm feeling pretty fragile, to tell you the truth,' she answered. 'Sorry if I was a bit vile yesterday, but as I tried to tell you, I've just got nothing to give.'

'Donna, I'm not asking you for anything. This is not about you having to give me anything. I know you're worried about Luke. I just wanted you to know I'm thinking of you, and I'm here if you need anything.'

She felt tears threatening to force their way down her face again, and she choked them back. She felt another wave of guilt, and she heard a slightly harsh tone in her voice when she replied, 'Thanks Patrick. I appreciate your call. But no, there's nothing you can do.' She was still struggling with the tears as she spoke. 'I'll give you a call some time, but I'm not much company right now. Bye.' She sighed. Too hard to put herself out on a limb. Besides, she needed every bit of her energy for Luke's plight.

Why did Patrick have to be so nice to her? Did she deserve that? Maybe she'd been a lousy mother, and that's what lay behind Luke's problems?

And then the war with tears was lost, and she found herself howling with a pain she couldn't compare with anything she'd ever felt before. Perhaps even more than when Martin had left. She just hoped her boy would be alright. That he'd be able to get his life back together. It was all such an awful mess.

Eventually the pain subsided. Maybe a warm bath would help to relax her, she decided. She went into the bathroom and started to run the water. While the tub filled she caught a glimpse of herself in the mirror. Dark rings under her eyes. Not her best look. She felt as if she'd aged ten years in the last few days.

A few minutes later she turned on a favourite piece of Elgar and lowered herself into the bath, letting Jacqueline du Pres and the warmth of the water soothe her. For a while she almost felt calm again, lying there until the water started to chill.

Donna dried herself and threw on a soft blue track-suit. She brushed her hair and made herself a cup of tea. Lady Grey. Just what she needed. She curled up in a comfortable chair in the lounge room, then picked up the phone and dialled.

'Hi Martin. Just wondered if you've got any time to call in for a while this afternoon?'

'I can be there in an hour.'

Donna knew he was the only one who would get it. She felt relief as she hung up the phone. For the time being it felt good to be able to have Martin there again. Even though it was just for a little while. But hopefully a little while was all she'd need.

~~

Martin sat opposite her, his silence questioning her.

'Sorry to call on you. It felt like you're the only one that can understand how all this feels.'

He looked at her for a while before answering, 'Sounds like you're not coping too well.'

'No. I feel helpless. I don't know what to do.'

'Donna, the truth is you *are* a bit helpless. We both are. Luke knows he has our support. We've done the groundwork, found a good place for him to be in. That's all we can do. This is one thing you can't fix for him. You always were inclined to do that. But this is something that Luke has to deal with. Essentially, he *is* on his own, apart from the professionals who'll be there to help him. But he has to do it himself. You can't do it for him. Neither can I.'

'He'll be okay, though, won't he?'

'I hope so. But you know, I can't say for sure. He's still in denial. Maybe he's ready. Maybe not. It's up to him now.'

Donna stared at him. She was wanting more re-assurance than that. But at the same time she knew he couldn't give it to her.

Martin sat quietly for a while. Then, looking right at her he said, 'You're stronger than you realise, Donna. And you don't *need* me. I know you feel you do at the moment. And we're in this together, and we'll support each other through this, but you don't need me in the way you think you do.'

She felt shocked to hear his words. But perhaps he was right. It had felt good to recapture a piece of their past. But it *was* the past. They could never re-create history.

She nodded 'I know.'

Chapter 30

'You're quiet. What's going on?' Halle asked Donna.

Donna was obviously not herself. She'd not spoken much throughout lunch, probably because she knew if she did she might get teary. She'd cried so often since Luke's admission into rehab, she wanted some time out from all the drama to just relax with her friends. She glanced at Trudy, who'd already heard it all. Trudy smiled and nodded, a nod that said "I'm here for you".

'It's been a rough couple of weeks. It's Luke. He's a real mess.' She filled them in on what had happened.

'How long ago did he go into rehab?' asked Nina.

'Just a week ago. He's been up and down, but he had a good day yesterday, so that's encouraging.'

'Did you know he was drinking?' asked Halle.

'No, not until he turned up to my place with alcohol on his breath one morning. But I've known something was up. He never used to go more than a week or two at the most without calling me. But he hadn't been contacting me, and he hadn't returned my calls lately either. Anyway, I know he's in the best possible place he can be.'

'Yeah, pretty distressing time for you though,' said Halle. 'God, Donna, you must be feeling like shit. I don't think anything gets to us like our children.'

Donna nodded. 'Yeah, it's been tough. But I'm feeling better than I did. Martin's been great, and it's been good to let go of those negative feelings I've been carrying about him for so long.' She laughed. 'I don't want to kill him any more. I've actually had some warm feelings towards him – God knows I never thought I'd feel anything like that again– and he's been a huge support. But he's telling me I need to stop feeling like I've got to fix it for Luke like I always have.' She turned to Trudy. 'Do you think I did that?'

'Donna, don't you remember? The only big row we ever had was when I told you to stop trying to rescue him and let him learn from consequences. Way back, when he was acting out at school. You got angry with me.

Donna stared at Trudy. 'I'd forgotten that.'

'You've always been a bit of rescuer, Donna,' said Nina. 'You're very protective.'

A rescuer? Donna had never seen herself like that. She gulped. It hurt. Okay. She took a deep breath, then laughed wryly. 'Well, this should be good for a few months therapy. Funny how we don't see ourselves the way others do sometimes.'

'We're here to be each others' mirrors,' said Nina. 'I would probably still be stuck with Tony if I didn't have you guys giving me a hard time about it.'

'Yeah, and I might have gone after the lap-band option. And just look at me now!' chuckled Paula. 'The weight's just dropping off me and I feel terrific.'

'And your new clothes look pretty damn good on you, too, by the way,' said Trudy.

'Yeah, it's been quite uplifting. I would never have believed what a new wardrobe could do for you,' smiled Paula. 'Thanks, Halle, for pushing me on that.'

'Well here's to a sensational group of women! Let's all promise to wear purple in style when we're old and live outrageous lives to the very end,' said Nina.

'You've got a few years on us,' added Halle. 'We'll be quirky old crones a long time before you.'

'Funny about age, isn't it?' said Nina. 'I know I'm the youngest of us, but I never think about it.'

At that moment the waitress approached their table with a bottle of Moet, compliments of Rick.

'Wow. What have we done to deserve this?' asked Donna.

Nina smiled. 'Well, let's just say I won't be joining you in a drink.'

'What are you saying?' asked Trudy. 'You're the piss-pot among us. If you're not drinking…'

'I'm pregnant.'

The women shrieked, obviously excited for their friend.

'Nina, that's brilliant,' said Trudy. 'I'm so thrilled for you.'

Nina's face was glowing. 'I couldn't wait to tell you guys.' She paused. 'But wait, there's more,' she added, joking.

'You mean you're having twins?' laughed Trudy.

'No. Rick and I are getting married. Can you believe it?'

'Wait, hang on a moment. I thought you were phobic about marriage,' said Paula.

'Yes, it seems true love won me over.'

'So…when?' asked Halle, throwing her arms around Nina. 'When's it all happening?'

'We're having a New Year wedding. Just a small one with our very closest friends and family. I've been busting to show and tell.'

'My God, Nina, when you take the leap of faith you sure do it quickly,' laughed Trudy. 'I'm so thrilled for you.'

Rick approached their table, his face beaming. He looked at Nina, silently querying if she'd broken the news.

'Yes, I've told them. Seems like they approve. You've saved me from their constant reprimands for my inappropriate life choices.'

'Glad to help,' Rick smiled, putting an arm around Nina's shoulders. He looked fondly at her.

'Rick, you're going to have to stop spoiling us with these beautiful wines you keep lavishing on us,' said Halle.

'Well if it weren't for all of you I probably would never have met Nina. And if not for loyal patrons like you I wouldn't have been able to develop Ricardo's.'

The champagne glasses had arrived at the table, and their host opened the bottle and poured.

169

Chapter 31

Beethoven's Pastoral symphony was drawing to a close. Donna breathed deeply. Just what she needed. She smiled at Patrick, seated beside her. He'd been quietly steadfast in his support, phoning every couple of days to check how she was going. When he'd called her last night he'd asked if she'd like to go to an MSO concert. Music had always been an elixir for her, and she'd decided to accept his invitation.

The audience's applause filled the auditorium. Donna felt relaxed. She was pleased she'd decided to come out tonight.

'That was beautiful,' she whispered to him.

He nodded. 'I always enjoy Beethoven. I can't say I got much from the Sculthorpe, though. I can't get my head around the more modern stuff.'

Donna smiled. 'I'm all for melody, I must admit. But the Beethoven and the Sibelius more than made up for the first half. You know, I'd forgotten how much I enjoy the MSO. Martin and I used to subscribe, but when he left he took custody of the tickets. And I just never got around to taking up a subscription again.'

Patrick laughed. 'Well, I have tickets for a couple more concerts. If you're interested we could go. I'll show you the program later.'

'That'd be great.'

They made their way out of the concert hall.

~~

'I don't know how you could have kept on being nice to me. I've been feral,' said Donna.

Patrick didn't answer immediately. He looked intently at her. Donna felt herself flush as she met his eyes in the dim light. They were sitting in Patrick's car, parked outside Donna's house.

'It didn't feel like you were being feral. I know how stressed you've been. I didn't want to be intrusive, but I just wanted to stay in touch. I know how hard it is to go through something like this.'

Donna looked at him. 'You sound like you've been there?'

He paused. 'Yes. My daughter. The one who's caught up in her career. She's been a pretty high-powered exec, you know, determined to break through the glass ceiling. And she did that. But she was mixing with a pretty fast crowd, and got into the high life. Cocaine. She eventually checked herself into rehab, and she's okay now. She's been clean for a couple of years. But I know how scary it can be to see your children in that situation.'

'Yeah.'

'So...you kept telling me you had nothing to give. But I wanted you to know I understood.' He paused. 'It's bloody tough.'

Donna nodded. 'Do you want to come in for a while?'

'Just for a while. You look like you could use a good night's sleep.'

Donna laughed. 'Great! Just what a woman likes to hear when she's out with a man. You'd better get some sleep because you look like shit.'

'Oh God no, that's not what I meant at all. I just know how wearing all that stress can be.'

Donna reached out and squeezed his hand. 'Thanks. You'll never know how much I appreciate your support.' She paused. 'Or your persistence. Anyway, let me make it up to you now with the best cup of coffee in Melbourne.'

'I'm up for that.'

~~

'My God,' laughed Patrick. 'Do you know what time it is?'

'Twelve o'clock?'

'It's one fifteen! Where the hell did the time go? Anyway, I'm going. Let you get that sleep I so rudely told you you needed.'

'It's been great. Thank you. And I'd love to go to those other couple of concerts you suggested.'

She walked him to the door, opening it and waiting expectantly to see whether she'd get the peck on the cheek again. There it was. Same polite kiss. He obviously wasn't interested in her that way. Or perhaps he was shy? After all, he did say he'd taken a long time to pluck up the courage to ask her for coffee the first time. She impulsively leaned forward and gave him a quick, soft kiss on the lips, then drew back, embarrassed. She looked at him, waiting to gauge his reaction.

Patrick smiled at her, a slow, slightly amused curl of the lips. He leaned forward and kissed her again, a more lingering kiss. 'Have you any idea how much I wanted to do that?' He looked directly into her eyes.

'I wasn't sure. I thought maybe you just wanted friendship. That you weren't interested in anything else. And I haven't exactly been encouraging, either.'

'I'm certainly interested. But I know you're pretty fragile at the moment. I've been feeling that what you're needing more than anything right now is my friendship.' He paused. 'How about we start there? The last thing I want to do is spoil things. We'll have plenty of time to see where this leads us.' Then he added, 'I haven't wanted to rush you.'

He was quiet for a moment. A smile broke across his face. Donna thought what a lovely face he had when he smiled.

'But don't think for one moment that I wouldn't love to take you up to the bedroom right now,' he said. 'You have no idea how much restraint I'm showing.'

It took Donna all her self-discipline not to say, "Stuff the restraint, let's go to bed." Instead, she just smiled at him. 'Goodnight. I'll look forward to seeing you soon.'

Chapter 32

The doorbell rang. Donna walked downstairs and let Martin in. It still sometimes felt odd. All those years it had been *their* place. She wondered what it must feel like for him. Probably even stranger. After all, this had been the house they'd built together. The place where they'd raised their children. Now he stood awkwardly in the hall, before Donna nodded in the direction of the study. How did it feel for him to need permission now to enter what used to be his favourite room? His man-cave.

They'd taken to catching up each week now. Initially it had been something they both needed, to talk about what was happening with Luke. And somehow it had developed into a habit. Every Tuesday morning, Donna's day off work. So natural and yet so unnatural, in their re-ordered world.

'Cup of tea?' she asked.

'Actually, I wouldn't mind a coffee. As strong as you can make it.'

She looked at him, surprised. He'd always been a tea drinker.

'I'm drinking more coffee these days,' he said.

She chuckled. 'Were you reading my thoughts?'

'I could see the look on your face.'

Donna went to the kitchen. She added an extra heaped scoop to the plunger. Would that be strong enough? She placed a small dish of Melting Moments and the coffee onto a tray and carried it into the study. The biscuits used to be Martin's favourites. She'd baked them yesterday. She wasn't sure why she'd bothered to do that. Did Trisha bake him Melting Moments? She wondered what their life was like.

Donna had always enjoyed giving him little surprises when they were married. Was she still trying to please him? Maybe he didn't even like Melting Moments any more.

He looked pleased. 'Thanks. You remembered.'

'I wasn't sure if you'd still like them. You know, strong coffee and eight years later.' She smiled.

'But some things never change, Donna.'

'What do you mean?'

Martin was silent. Donna looked at him, not sure if he intended to answer her.

After what felt like a very long time he said, 'Donna, I'm so sorry about hurting you. I've never been able to forgive myself.'

Donna stared at him.

'And I can talk about the proverbial time-of-life crisis. I suspect it was something like that. You know, being in my sixties, and the younger woman who flattered my aging ego. But I always missed our history, all the good, familiar things we shared for all those years.'

'And those years of familiarity became dull for you. But I'd never picked it up. I felt so stupid that I'd missed that.'

'God no, Donna. It was never about our marriage. We had a good marriage. It was never about you. It was me.' He paused, then added, 'So I tried to fix "me" with a younger woman. God, what a cliché! But it's true.'

He looked away, uncomfortable. 'I knew pretty soon what a terrible mistake I'd made. It didn't take long for the relationship with Trisha to lose its sheen. But I felt like I'd burned my bridges and couldn't turn back. So I've spent these past few years trying to make it work. Not fitting in with her friends. And feeling too ashamed to connect with ours…and missing you, and our life. Things like you knowing I loved Melting Moments, and your being able to know what I was thinking.'

Martin sat very still, staring at the carpet now. ' I know I've got no right to expect anything after all this time. I'm not expecting you to understand. But I wanted you to know I've never stopped loving

175

you.' Another pause. 'I've never stopped regretting what I'd done, and hoping one day you'd forgive me.'

Donna didn't answer immediately. She was stunned. She'd always assumed Martin had been able to move on without looking back. 'Why didn't you ever tell me this before?'

Martin looked right at her now. 'I'm not sure. I thought you must hate me for leaving you, that there was no point. But seeing you over these past few weeks has been very confronting. It hit me even harder what I lost when I walked away. It's been tough, of course, for both of us having to look at Luke struggling. But it threw us together again and made me take my head out of the sand and admit to myself all the things I'm saying to you today.'

Donna felt the tears rising. She didn't even try to push them away. She looked across at Martin, and saw that he, too, was moist around the eyes.

'I don't know what's happening in your life. I haven't wanted to ask Becky. I don't know if you've got someone else. But...but I've got to ask the question. I've ...often wondered if there's any way you'd consider us giving it another go?'

She didn't answer, but sat gazing into space. This felt just as surreal as the day he told her he was leaving. In the very early days she'd prayed for this to happen. But she'd stopped having any imaginings about it a long time ago.

Martin interrupted her thoughts. 'Spending all this time together over the last few weeks has brought up so many feelings. It's felt good to be able to remember what your little looks mean, to hear all those familiar expressions and relax into all our old ways. But so weird, too, to feel the chasm between us. Our two separate lives.'

Eventually Donna answered, haltingly. 'Martin, this is not what I was expecting. I can't answer you right now. I need time to digest this before I even begin to consider what you're asking me.'

'Yeah. I get that. I...I'm feeling quite overwhelmed myself. I...I should go.'

He got up and made his way towards the front door, Donna following close behind. Suddenly he turned, put his arms around her without speaking. For a moment Donna stood confused, her arms by her side. Then she tentatively put them around his waist. They stood together for some time. She felt his familiar, unfamiliar body next to hers. Then his arms fell to his side. He turned on his heels and left without looking back.

~~

A day had passed since Martin had dropped his bombshell. After a sleepless night filled with a myriad of thoughts, Donna called Trudy.

'I need a cup of coffee and your steadying influence.'

Now she sat in her friend's lounge room. 'My mind's mush.'

She relayed to Trudy what had happened.

'God, talk about a mega-surprise! I certainly wasn't expecting that! How are you feeling?'

'I haven't had a chance to untangle what I'm feeling yet. I've replayed it a thousand times since yesterday, but I'm still shell-shocked.'

'So am I. I don't know that you can expect any words of wisdom from me right now. Perhaps all I can do is ask questions. Like what the hell do you want to do? Would you consider giving it another go?'

Donna just sat shaking her head. 'I don't know. I'd given up considering it years ago. But I must admit there's something about the familiarity that's very tempting. You know, all those years of history. Of knowing how he thinks. Of him knowing how I think. There's something appealing about that. We always talked about this stage of our lives. Enjoying our grandchildren together. Travelling once we reached the empty nest stage.'

Trudy didn't answer.

After a moment Donna continued, 'And you know it's been incredible being able to just leave things to Martin again, with everything that's been happening with Luke. I'd forgotten what that was like. I've become so used to having to do it all myself.'

'Yeah...yeah, but is that all bad?'

'What do you mean?'

'Well, it's been fabulous to see you gradually start to believe in yourself over these years. To see you making decisions for yourself. You always used to seem confident when you were married, but I knew deep down you didn't feel as self-reliant as you appeared. And it's been great to see you becoming a person in your own right, rather than living in Martin's shadow.'

Donna was quiet, taking in what Trudy was saying. Then she said, 'Do you think I did that?'

Trudy nodded, adding, 'If you went back I'd like to see you do that because you still love Martin, rather than because you need him to prop you up. Or because you see him unhappy and want to fix it for him - again!'

Donna looked at Trudy, surprised. She still wasn't used to recognising her tendency to fix things.

'You've both been going through a crisis, and I'm sure it's been a relief to be able to rely on him. And of course familiar is great, too. But is it enough? You know I'd be the first to support you if you decide to go down that path. But it's about you deciding if it's because you want to be there or if it's just the easier way.'

'I don't know. I'm confused.'

'You need to give yourself time to decide. It's been more than eight years. You don't need to make any decisions straight away.'

'Yes, you're right. I don't, do I?' Then she picked up her bag. 'I'd better get going. Thanks again, Trude.'

Chapter 33

Donna looked around her garden. She was tired but contented, as she observed the flowers she'd just finished planting. She'd always enjoyed lots of colour. Martin was more of a shrubs and greenery man, and for years she'd gone along with that. 'No need to keep on putting time and money into all those annuals,' he'd always insisted. But now she was able to enjoy her pansies, petunias, impatiens and a host of other bright splashes of colour. Beautiful. She smiled to herself, an expression of her enjoyment.

Trudy had got her thinking yesterday. Perhaps she hadn't given enough consideration to how much she'd changed over these eight years. She'd certainly been aware of the blow to her confidence. But now she thought about how, once the raw pain had subsided, she'd gradually and almost imperceptibly re-established her life. Sometimes with great difficulty. But how different that life was! Oh yes, she'd made mistakes, all right. Some doozies. But when she thought about it, she didn't have too many regrets.

It had been comfortable being married to Martin. Comfortable and predictable. But maybe she'd become so used to the pattern of their life and acquiescing to what he wanted during their years together she *had* been prone to living in his shadow.

A yellow butterfly rested on one of her plants. She thought about the symbol of the butterfly, emerging from its chrysalis. She remembered the fable about the little boy who, in his efforts to help the butterfly in its struggles, actually thwarted its chances of flying. The butterfly needed the struggle to enable it. And like the butterfly, her own struggle had given her a new sort of resilience. She had even started to like the person she was becoming. *If* she did consider going back to Martin, would she be able to sustain those changes? Or would she be returning to some lesser version of herself?

She picked up the secateurs and went over to one of her favourite rose bushes, her Blackberry Nip, cutting three of the loveliest flowers to place in a vase inside. She took a deep breath, inhaling the scent and relishing their rich pinky-red hue. She walked towards the house, and realised she'd been singing.

As she strolled inside, she glanced at the sideboard in the dining room. Martin had chosen it from that shop in High Street all those years ago. She wasn't so sure she actually liked it any more. Maybe she'd get rid of it. Perhaps it was time for something more sleek and modern.

~~

Lunch was almost over. Donna had appreciated the opportunity to toss around her thoughts with her friends.

'You can't go back to him,' Nina had said crisply. 'He was a bastard to you. You deserve better. He didn't do the right thing by you. Why would you want to go back?'

Donna smiled to herself. It wasn't so long ago that Nina had been embroiled in her relationship with Tony, who'd certainly not treated her well. And that had not been the only toxic relationship her young friend had engaged in. Martin certainly couldn't be compared with any of them. Nina was underestimating the significance of the longevity of her time with him. And they were primarily good years, no doubt about that.

'I don't know that it's about Martin being a bastard,' Trudy argued. 'They've got a history. It's more about whether it would make Donna happy. Whether it would be the best thing for her, or whether the new path Donna's been on is actually more what she's needing now.'

Donna looked at Trudy. 'It's so interesting to hear you say that. I *have* gotten to enjoy the *un*familiar. Thrived on it.

'Well I think you've been brave,' said Paula. 'If I hadn't met Ted straight away I couldn't have done what you've done. Especially after what happened with Harvey. And then Art.'

'It's certainly been a challenge,' replied Donna. 'But you know, when I think about it, I gained something from the challenge. In a way I can't imagine going back to the way things were with Martin.'

'It wouldn't be the way things were,' said Halle.

'What do you mean?'

'You're not the same person. The relationship wouldn't be the same. Don't know if it would be better, or worse. But it would be different. You'd both be bringing your experience of eight years of life apart back into the relationship. In a way it'd be a new relationship, with an old partner.'

'Hm. I hadn't thought about it like that.'

'Anyway, what about Patrick? You seemed like you liked him,' asked Nina.

Donna felt herself flush. She was quiet for a moment, then answered, 'I actually do like him…a lot. It's complicated, and I've been feeling very confused. He's been unbelievably patient. I told him about what Martin suggested, and he wants me to take my time and be sure what I want to do. He's been badly bruised a couple of times, and he doesn't want any ghosts of the past getting in the way if we are going to give us a chance.' She paused. 'But I've been feeling like I owe it to Martin to seriously consider going back.'

'You owe it to yourself to work out what's best for you, Donna,' said Trudy. 'Martin made his choice eight years ago. I love him, you know that. Always will, even though it was a race who was going to murder him first, you or me, when he did that to you. But it's time to decide for *you*, now. You need to listen to both your head and your heart.'

181

Nobody spoke for a while, before Donna broke the silence. 'You're right, it's time for me to stop deciding for anyone else's sake and work out what I want for me.'

'I think you already know,' said Trudy.

Chapter 34

Donna buttered the toast and spooned the scrambled eggs onto it. The bacon was already done, crisp, just the way Luke liked it. She took the plate to the table.

'Thanks, Mum. You're a gem. But tomorrow you've got to let me get breakfast for you. You can't keep spoiling me like this. You know I've got a lot to make up to you.'

'You've already done that. It's so good to see you coming through everything the way you have.'

'Yeah, well now it's up to me to keep going. You know I'm always going to be an alcoholic.'

Donna knew this was true, but didn't want to hear it. She wanted to feel that the nightmare was over.

'But I'm determined to get my life back on track,' said Luke, as if hearing her fears. 'I don't know what shape that'll be, though. I doubt that Jacquie will have me back. I was pretty difficult to live with when she threw me out. And of course I have to find work again, too.'

Donna sighed, reflecting on how much uncertainty there was in his life, and knowing she could do nothing to make that better. 'Do you want to live here or in London?'

'I don't know. Depends on whether Jacquie is prepared to try again. I want to see whether we can resurrect our relationship. I called her last night and she's pretty negative at the moment. Can't say I blame her.'

'It might take time to rebuild the trust.'

'She's not sure she wants to even try. I know things were pretty awful. But I'm still hoping I'll be able to persuade her to give us another go.'

Donna wondered about what had happened during those "awful" times. She wanted to ask more about it. But another part of her didn't want to know. That was then and this was now. Maybe Luke would get around to telling her one day.

'Would she consider coming back to Melbourne if you do get back together?'

'I doubt it. She's got her job over there and loves it. In the unlikely event that we can patch things up I don't know if she'd want to leave London. So I've talked to a couple of people here, putting out feelers about what might be available if I don't go back. If the relationship is over, which is highly probable, there's no reason I shouldn't stay here. I'm going to speak to Bernard later today about whether there might be a position for me back at Hill & Jamieson.'

'Don't forget Dad and Becky are coming for lunch. Can you make it later in the afternoon?'

'Yes, I told him I'd come into the office around four.'

Donna nodded. She felt a little excited. Of course she wanted things to work out well for Luke, and for him to be happy. But if his relationship was over it would be so good to have him back home again.

~~

Donna placed the last of the tapas on the platter, put them on the kitchen table, where she'd set up for lunch, and checked the soup on the stove. All ready. Luke was making his way downstairs. Just waiting for the rest of her family to arrive now. She thought she heard Becky turning the key in the lock. Then she heard Martin's voice; he'd obviously arrived right behind her.

'Why don't you all just come on in,' she joked. They were already in the kitchen with her.

'I just followed Becky in, she had a key,' said Martin apologetically.

'It's okay, I'm just teasing.'.

He handed her a bunch of roses he'd brought with him. It felt so strange having him bring flowers again after all these years.

'Thanks Marty.' She gave him a peck on the cheek. 'I've got lunch ready. I've made soup. Make yourselves comfortable, I'll dish it up in a minute.'

'What sort of soup are we having?' asked Becky.

'Pumpkin and ginger.'

'Yum. Let's start. I'm starving. I didn't have breakfast this morning because I had to get Maddy to the bus. She's gone on a school excursion.'

'Where's she going?' asked Donna.

'Her class is going to the Science Museum.'

Donna smiled. Her little girl was growing up. She went to the stove and stirred the soup.

'Can I help?' asked Luke.

'Yeah, you could put these flowers in a vase. And there's some crusty bread just warming in the oven. Can you take it out and slice it? Just pop it into that basket.'

It felt so good to have Luke there helping, and he obviously was enjoying it too. He'd decided to live with her until he'd worked out his plans. He looked at her and smiled. She loved that smile; it said so much.

She carried the soup to the table. 'Okay, let's eat,' she said, placing the bowls in front of everyone.

Donna looked around the table. The family unit re-assembled. She felt like Mother Hen again. She caught Martin's eye and he smiled.

'This is delicious. But you always were a good cook,' he said.

'I didn't do much cooking for a long time. I'm only just getting back into it.'

Martin looked guilty. He obviously got the link, understanding she'd stopped cooking when he left. Donna saw his discomfort, and recognised her impulse to say something reassuring. The rescuer in action. But she stopped herself, and said nothing. Tick! She'd been working on that with Norm; she would tell him about this minor achievement next week.

Donna looked around the table. The conversation had become more vibrant. It felt so good to see Luke in a better space. Some days he got moody, but he was gradually getting things together. It was a month now since he'd left rehab. And he and Becky were obviously relishing having time together. They'd always been so close, and she knew Becky loved having him back home. 'This feels so nice,' she said.

'Yeah, the old family, all grown up and back together again,' laughed Luke. 'Although I can't say I've been so grown up in recent times. But this is feeling fantastic. I've missed it.'

Martin met Donna's eyes. Family time. Reunited after all the years of being apart. He had put his heart on the line in his suggestion to Donna. If they got back together there'd be many occasions like this. Just like old times.

~~

Becky had left to go shopping. Maddy, her oldest, was having a birthday next week, and she'd gone to get a present for her. Luke had gone into the city to talk to the guys at his old law firm. That left her alone with Martin. They were loading the last of the dishes into the dishwasher.

'Want some extra strong coffee?' she asked.

'Thanks.'

'I don't want to offer you a drink. We might not be finished when Luke gets home, and I don't want to put that sort of temptation in front of him.'

'Yeah, eventually he'll have to live with other people drinking, but it's early days yet. Anyway, coffee's great.'

He was quiet. After a few minutes he said, 'It was special today.'

'Yes. I knew you felt that. We all did. That's the first time we've all been together for more than eight years. It's been a long time.'

'I'd like it to be like that for the rest of our lives. I've tried not to pressure you, but I need to ask. Have you thought about us any more?'

Donna took a deep breath and looked at him. His face looked anxiously alert. She spoke slowly.

'Yes, I've thought about it a lot. And I can see how good it feels to be together again. It always was good. Today showed me what things could be like again.' She hesitated. 'But...but we're not the same two people who were married all those years ago. I don't want to come back because it feels comfortable.'

Martin stared at her. 'So you're saying no?'

She nodded. 'I'm saying no.'

She knew there was a part of her that screamed in opposition to her decision, but she ignored it. 'I hate to disappoint you. I'll always love you. You've been such a major part of my life. But it's a different love now. It's like I've started a new chapter, and I can't go back to the old. I don't believe we can reconstruct our past. Too much has happened.' Donna paused, looking to see Martin's reaction. She wished he didn't look so sad.

'You're managing okay on your own?' he asked.

'Yes, it's been challenging at times. But I'm doing well.'

'Have you been dating?'

She nodded.

'How's that been for you? After all those years. I don't know if I'd have the courage to go it alone.'

'Yes, it felt weird at first. But it's okay.' She paused. 'You know, one of the men I've been out with not too long ago called me Donna Quixote.'

'What did he mean?'

'It certainly wasn't meant to be a compliment. He was telling me to stop being a dreamer. But I'm starting to like that part of me. And I'm learning, through some whopping big mistakes, to discover what's a dream and what's real. I'm sure I'll tilt at a few more windmills yet.' She laughed. 'But I need to embrace this experience and live it through the new person I'm becoming.'

Martin sat very still, staring somewhere, deep in thought. Then he looked at her. 'I'm proud of you.' He hesitated, and added, 'Of course, I wish you'd decided differently. But I didn't expect you would.' He was gazing out the window, saying nothing. Then he looked back at her. 'Do you remember I told you a few weeks ago you didn't need me in the way you thought you did? It turns out I was right.'

Donna walked over to him, a tear running down her cheek, and hugged him. They stood together for a while, then he said, 'I think I'd better go now.'

Donna nodded. They hugged again before she closed the door behind him.

Chapter 35

It was a perfect day. Not too hot like some January days could be, with the trees providing just enough dappled sun filter. Donna was pleased she'd offered to have Nina and Rick's wedding at her place. They'd thought about having it at the restaurant, but were thrilled she'd offered her home. As they'd wanted, it was to be a small gathering, with just twenty-four people to help them celebrate their union.

Three tables were set around the garden, which looked lush and colourful, the setting enhanced by the scent of the summer flowers. The late afternoon ceremony was to be held right to one side of the garden, next to her roses. Donna was grateful it wasn't raining.

Halle was busy with last minute arrangements, talking to the chef from Ricardo's who, with his team of helpers, now filled Donna's kitchen. Halle had offered to coordinate the arrangements for the wedding and Donna could see why her friend excelled in her work; she had everything at her fingertips and made it all seem so easy. She was now organising the placement of tea lights for the festivities once the sun set, the lighting was organized throughout the garden and some outdoor heaters were already positioned in case the air temperature grew cool. Flowers and candles adorned the tables, bright yellow as requested by Nina. A harpist had also been engaged to play as the guests arrived. The waiters were set to go, and now Donna could just get herself ready and wait for the bride and groom, the celebrant and guests to arrive.

She felt a little nervous about whether everything would go well today. She went upstairs to get herself dressed.

~~

Nina wore a flowing cream, bias-cut satin dress that revealed the slight curve of her belly. She looked more conservative than any of them had ever seen her, but she'd told them, 'This is one day you'll see a more traditional me. I can go as crazy as I like any other day of my life. But this one is special.' Her mad red curls were as wild as ever, though - Nina would always be Nina.

Rick's son, David, the only other member of the bridal party, looked excited about the responsibility of the job allocated to him. He was beaming from ear to ear as he stood waiting for the ceremony to begin. And Rick, who admitted to a few pre-wedding butterflies, nevertheless looked the proudest man on the planet as he stood next to his bride-to-be.

For a moment, just before the ceremony began, Donna noticed a look of panic on Nina's face. She looked like she was about to cry. But then the bride-to-be looked at Rick, who reached towards her and squeezed her hand, smiling; Donna saw with relief how the tension on her friend's face visibly dissipated.

Donna wiped away a tear. For a moment she was remembering her own wedding day, more than thirty-six years ago. The dreams for their future she'd had on that occasion. She'd never have considered that she and Martin wouldn't be together for the rest of their lives. She looked again at Nina and Rick, and hoped that their vision for the future would be fulfilled.

The celebrant began. She spoke of the sacred significance of the occasion. The joy and synchronicity of Nina and Rick finding each other. The life they could look forward to spending together. Then Nina and Rick spoke the carefully prepared words of their marriage vows. The ceremony was beautiful.

And then it was over. Nina was a married woman! She looked across at her friends with a look that said, "We did it. I bet you never thought this would happen."

The guests made their way to the tables, and the waiters were soon busily bringing food to them. Donna smiled at the drink waiter who'd appeared next to her, and nodded that she would like a glass of wine. The staff were doing a great job. It was good to feel that things were being taken care of, and she could just sit back, relax and enjoy herself. She looked around the garden at the guests. They looked like they were enjoying themselves.

She'd been thrilled that Nina had invited Becky, James and Luke, especially since she and Rick had only a small number of guests.

Suddenly her body stiffened. The waiter had poured drinks for Becky and James, and now had the bottle poised above Luke's glass. He was deeply engrossed in conversation with Becky, and the waiter poured the wine. Donna felt nauseous, fearful he'd succumb to the temptation. It took all her constraint not to whisk the glass away. Don't drink it darling, her heart cried out to him, as if her thoughts could will him.

Luke finished his conversation with his sister, and saw the wine in front of him. He paused briefly, reached his hand towards the glass, then quietly pushed it towards Becky. Turning to the waiter, he asked, 'Could I have some mineral water, please?'

Donna sighed. Thank God. She sat back. Would she ever again feel worry free? She could only hope that Luke would have the resources to combat his alcoholism. He caught her eye, sensing what had just transpired for her. He leaned across, and whispered, 'It's alright Mum. I'm okay.'

She breathed a deep sigh of relief.

'You've got to trust me,' he said.

She nodded.

~~

Donna stood to one side of the festivities, reflecting with pleasure now on the vibrancy of the occasion. She was delighted with how the day had flowed. The ceremony, the dinner, the speeches and the general ambience were just as she'd hoped.

Her thoughts were interrupted by Rick's brother calling for everyone's attention for the cutting of the cake. Donna made her way over to where it was placed on a table, under her favourite Japanese Maple, located in one corner of the garden.

Nina and Rick stood ready, caught in a fragment of time, looking at each other. She had her hand on her belly. Rick had his arm around her shoulder. There was a peace to Nina in that moment that Donna hadn't seen before. A look that said she'd arrived at a place that had eluded her for so long.

Trudy was standing next to Donna, and whispered, 'What a beautiful day. Couldn't have been better. Wouldn't Gina would have loved it?'

'Yes, she would. I'm thrilled with the way it's all gone. And so happy for Nina.'

~~

The guests were gone, and everything had been cleared. Donna sat quietly now, alone in her lounge room. Luke was asleep upstairs, and the house felt still. She kicked off her shoes, freeing her feet from the constraints and pain of the very high heels that she was not used to wearing these days.

The phone rang. She hoped it might be Patrick.

'Hi. How did it go?'

She smiled as she heard his voice. 'Just beautiful. Every bit as well as I could have hoped.' She told him all the details she could remember, and he listened, asking questions.

'You must be tired. It's late there now,' she said.

Patrick had had to fly to New Zealand to consult with one of his clients and was unable to get back in time for the wedding. She knew how disappointed he'd been, and was pleased he'd called as soon as he thought the wedding celebrations were over to check in with her.

'I am pretty tired. It's been a big day. But worthwhile. I'll tell you all about it when I fly in tomorrow.'

'Would you like me to pick you up from the airport? What time are you getting in?'

'My plane's due at eleven. But aren't you going to catch-up with Martin?'

'I'll cancel. We'll skip it until next week.'

'Okay, thanks, that'd be great. See you tomorrow.'

Donna hung up. She was also tired, but still stimulated with the aftermath of the day. She wasn't ready to go to bed yet. She poured herself a Bailey's and sat curled on the couch. She sent a text to Martin, letting him know she wouldn't make it in the morning. They'd continued to meet regularly, each of them valuing and enjoying their new type of bond. And when he'd decided to leave Trisha a couple of months ago, it had felt comfortable and natural for her to support him through that. She'd even encouraged him to consider trying One Plus One when he was ready to start dating. Like her, he'd initially been shocked at the idea.

'What, at *my* age? That's for young people!' he'd protested.

Donna, now the voice of experience, had laughed and reassured him that he was not past it at all.

She hadn't noticed time passing as she sat now, reflecting on the wedding, her re-formed relationship with Martin, and the shape of her life. Eventually she glanced at the clock and, seeing with surprise that it was after midnight, decided she'd better get to bed.

Chapter 36

The women had all had a turn to hold Carly, who now was quietly asleep in her pram in the corner, next to their usual table at Ricardo's. Nina glanced across at her from time to time, obviously enjoying her maternal role. She was glowing.

'How many months old is she now?' Paula asked. 'I lose track of time.'

'Seven months next week,' replied Nina.

'Is she always this good?' asked Paula.

'Most of the time. Mind you, she can get quite feisty like me if she's tired or hungry. But we're past the sleep deprivation phase, thank God. And Rick's a pretty hands-on Dad when he's not here working, so I'm hoping that it won't be long before I'll be able to get dirty with paint again. I'm aiming for another exhibition next year some time if I can get my shit together.' She laughed. 'Life sure changes, doesn't it?'

'Yeah. But thank goodness for the changes. Even with the troughs along the way,' said Donna.

'Talking of which, how's Luke doing now?' asked Paula.

'He's doing well. He had a relapse after Jacquie let him know there was no chance of them ever reconciling; but since then it's all been good. He's coming up for one year sober soon.'

'That's fantastic. How's he settled into his apartment?' asked Paula.

'Really well. He's been more house proud than I expected, and he's even surprising himself with how well he's managing.'

'I suppose you pop in there often?' asked Paula.

'Well actually, no, I'm trying not to get into the habit of being Mother Hen. I know it's best for him to manage things himself.' She laughed. 'But I have to admit sometimes I have to fight with myself not to get on the phone to see if I can help. I'm resisting the temptation, though.'

'Good,' said Trudy.

'And he's let me know he doesn't need me to do that, anyway.'

'Of course!' said Trudy. 'He's quite capable of managing his life now.'

'Pity Halle couldn't make it today,' said Nina. 'Do you know how the move to Sophia's house is going?'

'I think it's almost done. And she was telling me that Tilly has even been lending a hand,' said Trudy. 'She seems to have finally gotten over her tantrums.'

'About bloody time,' said Nina.

'I didn't get around there to help Halle as much as I would have liked,' said Trudy. 'I had another assignment to get in to Uni. God, talk about a love/hate relationship. I don't know which end is up half the time.'

'Yeah, but you're loving the H1's,' laughed Donna.

'That's true. Makes it all worthwhile. Just eats up the hours, though. Remember when I was complaining I didn't know what to do with my time?' She laughed. 'I'm sure the days have shrunk by a few hours.'

'Be careful what you wish for...' said Nina.

'Maybe I should find something like that,' said Paula. 'You know, I've always wanted to try art classes. I've noticed the CAE have got some courses going.'

Nina was thoughtful. 'I might even start some art classes myself. You could come along to them.'

'Sounds great,' Paula replied.

~~

The candles had almost burned down. Donna and Patrick had had a long, leisurely dinner.

'That was beautiful, as usual,' he said.

He enjoyed her meals, which made her renewed culinary interest even more gratifying. They'd already hosted a couple of dinner parties together, and both got a lot of pleasure from their mutual love of good food. Over dinner that night they'd talked about doing one of the gourmet walking tours he'd mentioned the first time they'd had coffee together. Probably in France, they'd decided, as they'd perused the options. They planned to travel through Europe for six weeks. The walking tour was to be one part of the total experience. That evening they'd chatted about plans for the places they'd like to visit.

'I can't wait to see Paris again. And for you to show me some of those wonderful places like Cinque Terre you've talked about. But I'm going to have to get fit before then. My bones are a bit creaky at the moment,' said Donna.

'It's okay, you've got a couple of months yet.'

She nodded. 'This is so exciting. I keep feeling like if I pinch myself I'll find it's all been a dream.'

Patrick laughed. 'Well, we're both part of the same dream. Can't be all bad.'

Donna felt relaxed and happy. 'This has all been so worth waiting for.'

'You mean the trip?'

'No, I mean you. Us.'

'Yes, it has been worth the wait,' he agreed. He gently stroked her cheek.

She looked intently at him, enjoying the softness of his features. He reached over and took her hand, then kissed her. Donna breathed a contented sigh.

She thought back now to those early months. Although she'd been very drawn to Patrick, she'd found herself vacillating between desire and doubt. She realised now she'd been afraid to trust her own judgement after her earlier disastrous choices. But she was grateful that Patrick had persevered. He'd patiently held their friendship together over that time. She was pleased now they'd taken it slowly. And here they were, approaching nine months. Their relationship had deepened since those early days and they were both now committed to a future together.

'It's going to keep getting better,' said Patrick. He smiled and squeezed her hand.

Donna nodded. They sat in silence, not needing words.

~ ~

Donna was sitting in her garden. She'd found a packet of Lapsang Souchong tea that had been given to her by Halle, and had decided to try it. It was a warm day, and she scanned the floral mix of colour, enjoying the peace that was only broken by the bark of a dog a couple of houses away.

She decided she didn't really enjoy the flavor of the tea; she placed the cup on a small table next to her, and picked up an old photo album she'd found that morning in one of her drawers. She hadn't looked at the album for years.

She turned to the first page and saw a young version of herself smiling back at her. How old would she have been then? Probably about thirty? She felt a momentary wave of empathy for her younger self. She could see traces of her insecurity behind the smiling face. Not that most people would have known. On the surface she knew she'd appeared much more confident than she really was. But Trudy knew; her friend had always understood her so well, and recognised that what you saw wasn't necessarily the full story. She'd seen that Donna had lived in Martin's shadow.

Donna had thought she was independent. She knew now, though, how reliant she'd really been on her husband during their marriage; she'd almost felt like a symbiotic extension of him. So when he'd left her, she'd felt like there was nothing remaining to live for. She shuddered now, reflecting on the desperation that had driven her to swallow those pills. She could scarcely believe that the Donna back then was the same person.

She couldn't help wondering, what if Martin had not left her? How would her life have panned out? Would she still be that self-doubting woman she'd just seen smiling out of that photo from the past? And did she regret the path her life had taken? Donna decided that she would not change anything. She knew that those belated rites of passage, her encounters with Harvey and Art, and the other aspects of her evolving life after Martin, had led her to where she was now. At peace, more whole, and with a man she loved.

She continued to turn the pages of the album, perusing family photos for perhaps half an hour, reflecting on life, then and now. The dog had stopped barking. Perhaps its sympathetic owner was now holding it or placating it with a bone. The garden was very quiet.

The doorbell rang, interrupting the moment. Donna stood up and walked inside. She knew that would be the Real Estate agent she'd called about selling her house. She paused on the way to the front door, looking around the home she'd lived in for more than thirty years. She knew it was time for change. She took a deep breath and opened the front door.